BEST
WOMEN'S EROTICA
2014

BEST
WOMEN'S
EROTICA
2014

Edited by

VIOLET BLUE

CLEiS
PRESS

Published in the United States by Cleis Press, Inc., 2246 Sixth Street, Berkeley, California 94710.

Printed in the United States.
Cover design: Scott Idleman/Blink
Cover photograph: Yulia.M/Getty Images
Text design: Frank Wiedemann

First Edition.
10 9 8 7 6 5 4 3 2 1

Trade paper ISBN: 978-1-62778-003-2
E-book ISBN: 978-1-62778-016-2

"Blame *Spartacus*," by Laura Antoniou, first appeared in D. L. King's *Under Her Thumb: Erotic Stories of Female Domination* (Cleis Press, 2013). "Chattel," by Errica Liekos, first appeared in Rachel Kramer Bussel's *Serving Him* (Cleis Press, 2013). "Close Shave," by Alison Tyler, will appear in her anthology *Nine-to-Five Fantasies: Tales of Sex on the Job*.

CONTENTS

INTRODUCTION: NEVER TOO FAR

The *Best Women's Erotica* series began in 2000. I took over the series as editor in 2005 and found that I'd inherited guardianship of a friskily forward-thinking millennial.

I've edited *Best Women's Erotica* for nearly a decade. Every year, I receive as many as 300 submissions—meaning I've read somewhere near 3,000 hopeful erotic stories for the series alone. *Best Women's Erotica* has also won its share of awards over the years under my hand, with honors ranging from gold to bronze. A few authors have managed to be published at both ends of that near-decade.

> "I can see now that I made a mistake," her husband said. "You don't need your freedom, do you? You need to know you're wanted. You need to know you're loved."
>
> Sasha felt her legs go weak. She leaned on Alex, and he held her weight. There were no windows in

their front hall. She opened and closed her eyes to the same solid black.

"I'll be clear from here on out. You're mine. I own you. I tell you to spend time with your friends because it gives me pleasure to do so. Because I like you missing me, and I like it when you come home with new stories from your friends and your world to entertain me. I expect you to stay independent and entertaining to me. Do you understand?"

Sasha nodded.

"Because I have no interest in owning something weak and unchallenging, Sasha. I want you strong and I want you to have your own interests." Alex lowered his voice even more. "But you belong to me. Do you understand?"

Sasha nodded again.

"I'm not sure you do. Go into the living room. I'm going to show you."

—Errica Liekos, "Chattel"

Including this edition—my ninth—I've published 173 erotic stories written by female authors from several cities in Australia (including Victoria and Sydney), many locations in England (including London, Brighton and Surrey), Germany (Berlin), the Netherlands, many places in Canada (like Toronto and Vancouver), France (Paris), New Zealand, India (New Delhi), Vietnam, a few locations in Scotland (Glasgow and Edinburgh), Ireland, Spain, Russia, Mexico (Mexico City), and nearly half of all the United States, from Hawaii to Brooklyn, New York.

He returns her surly stare with his own. I notice how his eyes look suddenly smoky in the intensity of the moment. Abby can make things get serious in a heart-beat. My girlfriend has that way about her that tells everyone she lives in a no bullshit zone. She's smirking now. "See this is my problem. Marcella thinks I fuck like a girl."

"Abby!" I can't believe how she blurted that out.

Abby folds her arms. "Do you want to help her make a comparison?"

"Oh my god!" I gasp, hiding behind my hands.

Abby plows forward despite my mortification. "This is the last class tonight. I can lock the door."

Brett doesn't look shocked. Even if he is, he's way too cool for that. He looks amused. "You want me to do your girlfriend. Right here."

—Alyssa Turner, "Reality TV"

Even though it hails from women all over the world, the series has become a lens through which to view the direction of mainstream Western female sexuality. *Best Women's Erotica* has been able to stay ahead of erotic trends by being both nimble and unafraid—I've simply been publishing the best erotic fiction I've found (with the requirement that it be superbly written and include plenty of hardcore sex). It makes people ask me what I think women's sexual fantasies are, why women sometimes want to dominate or be dominated, and what it is, exactly, that "women want."

"I'll just put this down here, shall I?" he said, gesturing with his head in the direction of the antique dresser. His accent was more rainy Manchester than romantic Sorrento, but it didn't take the level of my filthy fantasizing down even a notch.

I just nodded, barely noticing that Mitchell had returned to the room and was already fumbling in his wallet for a no doubt hefty tip. Not that he needed to buy this man's silence. The expression on the waiter's face told me that not only did he like what he saw very much indeed, but also that this wasn't the first time he'd interrupted some explicit scene or other. After all, the Charmont prided itself on its discretion as a venue, and you didn't hang on to that kind of reputation for long if you employed staff who didn't know when to keep their mouths shut.

He left the room with slow, backward steps, taking one last good look at my naked curves and the submissive posture in which they were displayed. Even before the door shut behind him, Mitchell was unbuckling his belt and pulling it free of his trouser loops.

—Elizabeth Coldwell, "In Threes"

Explicit erotica authored by and for women, as it turns out, refuses to be pinned down into neat categories—and nothing has infuriated writers for women's magazines more when they've asked me what the series means for "what women really want [in bed]." What it means, I tell them, is that what women want is high-quality porn woven into their high-quality fiction, and every year we break new taboos in our shared quest for thrills and satisfaction. And if the stories in this collection are indeed a barometer for the range of lovemaking, masturbation and fucking that women fantasize about, in a dizzying and sometimes shocking range of fantasies and combinations, then this quest is deliciously never-ending.

Don't let this lead you to believe the negative stereotype that we women can't make up our minds when it comes to sex. The women who write these stories know exactly what they want. Our readers do, too. I know this because they tell me, more women than I can count; in every way they can communicate to me, the readers let me know what they think, all the time, consistently and without fail. I listen, and engage readers at every chance they give me. The women who read these steamy stories and use them to the fullest also use the literate porn they find between these pages (and pixels) as yes-no-maybe laundry lists of sexual fantasies.

> I found myself an isolated corner and began to read a historical romance novel. The prose was clean and virginal, so I filled in the dirty parts in my head. After a few wild fantasies, I became completely aroused, and decided to head home to the privacy of my dorm for a bit of self-love. A sudden rainstorm prevented me from taking the long walk home, so I scanned the library.
>
> I found the perfect spot: it was secluded, yet still in the open. Anyone could have stumbled upon me, skirt yanked up, fingers inside my panties as I brought myself to a toe-curling orgasm. It was a life changing-experience, so thrilling and naughty. I was hooked from that moment.
>
> —Oleander Plume, "Out in the Open"

Yet as much as this series is clearly, er, *useful* for so many women, the thing I've not yet felt the pundits and magazines are willing to admit is something that has become very obvious for me and the authors I've published over the decade here. It's that once women uncork the possibilities of what they like in sexual fantasy and fetish erotica, they don't stop at the first story that works for them. We keep going, and no, it doesn't get old because we keep looking for more to turn us on and get us off—which is exactly what this series sets out to do.

> The table beneath me is warm, but the food presented on my naked skin is not. A rainbow of sashimi is fanned across my belly: salmon, tuna, mackerel and yellowtail. Across my ribs is an array of sushi. Between my breasts are cuts of eel, drizzled with rich teriyaki sauce. And carefully arranged around my nipples are clutches of salmon roe, the eggs vibrant and bursting. Soft purple orchids frame my sex, and in the diamond formed by my spread and angled legs is a painted flask of warm sake.
>
> I breathe slowly, shallowly, so as not to disturb the presentation of food. The smell is intoxicating and I long for a bite of fish, the tingle of ginger and wasabi on my tongue. But for now I am merely a decoration, an attractive display for the artfully arranged delicacies. In other rooms, other girls are bound as I am, their bodies serving the same erotic aesthetic. From somewhere I can hear the melancholy notes of a *shamisen* being played by one of the hostesses.
>
> —Rose de Fer, *"Nyotaimori"*

This edition of *Best Women's Erotica* is a luscious example of what it looks—and feels—like when we demand more, more, more and richer, more sublime than the last. When going too far is just enough to tip us over the edge into taboo orgasmica. And what it's like when we try on the nastiest, filthiest sexual fantasies only to change into a romantic romp later, knowing we always wind up safe at home after our trip to the dirty movies in our minds.

I hope you find this year's collection as much of a wild ride— and sometimes, an erotic homecoming—as we have on this side of the manuscript.

Warm wishes,
Violet Blue
San Francisco

OUT IN THE OPEN

Oleander Plume

It's only 7:00 a.m., and my panties are already damp.

I lock myself into the tiny unisex bathroom and slip them off over my sandals, then wad them into a ball and stuff them into the bottom of my backpack. My long skirt flows around my bare skin as I step back out into the public eye. The coffee shop is almost deserted today. Kind of disappointing, really. Less people around not only lowers the risk, but gives me less fodder for my fantasies. Then I realize it's still early; the morning rush hasn't begun. So, I stay.

"One large café mocha, please."

The girl behind the counter has large, vacuous eyes and blood-red nail polish on her long fingernails. She looks bored. As I look at her, I wonder about her sexual appetites. Does she prefer to be on top, in control and dominant? Is she capable of multiple orgasms? Then, the question that always follows these random musings. Does she masturbate? I picture her leaning against the counter, pulling up her short denim skirt, and fingering her swollen clit. Her red nails shimmer under the fluorescent lights as she wriggles in bliss.

"Anything else?" Her soft voice snaps me back to earth.

"No thanks."

As she prepares my order, my eyes bounce around the room. I see a man in a perfectly tailored business suit, sipping a cup of black coffee as he reads the newspaper. My pondering begins again. Is he married? Does he have a satisfying sex life? He doesn't look like the type who would masturbate, but I'm sure he does. I imagine him behind a large, expensive desk, fly undone, stroking his thick cock with quick jerks while he watches porn on the Internet. My mouth waters, and my hunger grows. I imagine the look on his face as he reaches orgasm, eyes shut tight, wet lips open. Afterward, he cleans up with a pristine, white handkerchief as he hums a country song.

"Here's your mocha." I shiver when her hand lightly brushes mine as she hands me my order.

"Thanks."

I sit at a table in a far corner, facing the door. Two more people enter the shop: an older man, and a middle-aged woman wearing a business suit with sneakers. Commuters, only here for a fleeting moment before they head off to toil the day away, fueled by caffeine. Neither of them notices me. It's not that I'm forgettable; it's just that I have learned the fine art of blending in. I can become part of the landscape, so entwined with it that I'm almost like a piece of furniture. Hiding in plain sight is not only a survival mechanism; it's also a very helpful aspect to my hobby.

The shop has free wi-fi, so I pull out my laptop and get it set up. I enter the password for my blog and feel myself starting to drip. The excitement is almost too much to bear sometimes. My blog is the newest aspect of my naughty little pastime but has quickly become part of my daily routine. Being a part-time college student far from home, I have many free hours to fill. I sip my café mocha as I wait for the page to load. The businessman I had been watching earlier folds his newspaper neatly, then leaves the shop. The sneaker-footed woman claims his vacant chair. She looks so stressed, her lips pursed as she furiously sends a text. My mind puts together a complicated scenario for her as I begin to type.

There is a woman sitting across from me. Buttoned up, all business. What is she like when she lets her hair down? I'll bet she likes it in the ass. I can almost see her, bent over, plump round butt in the air, shivering with lust as she waits to be taken. She might even like a little spanking first. After he makes her ass nice and pink, her lover pours massage oil between her spread cheeks and then rubs it into her hungry hole as she mewls like a cat in heat. She longs to be stuffed with cock, and her lover obliges. While he fucks her back door, she sucks his fingers.

Seeing the words in my head come to life on the screen is almost surreal. I hit the enter key, publishing my dirty thoughts for the world to see. Anonymously, of course.

My screen name is Mischievous Mindy, and my blog is called *The Wet Panty Chronicles*. I have over a thousand followers, all filthy minded individuals who are captivated by my silly little hobby. My fingers fly over the keyboard.

She's wearing bright-red lipstick. I wonder if it ends up on her boss's dick. At the end of the day, his cock probably looks like a throbbing, dripping candy cane. Do you think she swallows? I do. Underneath that Talbot's suit, she's all slut, just waiting for her next taste of cock. I'll bet she likes her hair firmly tugged as she slurps down a mouthful of hot semen. Afterward, she licks her fingers and smiles.

By now I'm completely worked up, but I make myself wait.

The time isn't right, since the morning crowd has gotten thicker. My last entry has already received a thumbs up from one of my readers. It turns me on that someone is out there, pouring over my words and possibly masturbating while they do so. I turn my attention to a young man that is waiting for a large order. He looks twitchy and nervous. I imagine he is the new office boy for a team of horny executives.

Anxious coffee boy shifts from foot to foot as he waits in line. I wonder why he is so uptight. Is he afraid of getting the order wrong? What will happen back at the office if he does? Will he have to suck his boss's dick?

"I said low fat, bitch!" the lawyer growls, as he pushes his cock against the boy's soft lips.

"Sorry, sir," the boy will mumble as he fights back a smile. Two more partners walk in and he is stripped naked, then fondled by all the men, much to his great delight.

I have to stop and take a large gulp of my mocha before I can continue. In the meantime, sneaker woman leaves, and another takes her place. This one is younger and wears high-heeled pumps. Her legs are shapely.

A new woman is in my line of sight. Young, in professional attire. Her size-eight feet are stuffed into size-seven red heels. She smells like cheap body spray, and her eyes dart around nervously. Maybe she's meeting someone here, an older man perhaps?

As my words fill the blank space on the screen, the shop door opens and a man in a black suit enters. His eyes light up when he joins her at the table. Wedding band, slightly gray at the temples. My mind speeds up as I think of their story.

Bingo! He just showed up, married, guilty eyes, dirty mind. She is rubbing her knee against his under the table, trying hard to be coquettish, but she comes across as cheap and desperate. I'll bet when they're fucking, she calls him Daddy.

"Fuck me harder, Daddy!" she'll moan as he bends her over the bed in their cheap motel room. Maybe he tells her she's a naughty girl, then smacks her ass while he drills her wet slit. She looks like the type who would like that. Former cheerleader, she probably had a crush on the football coach, which started her obsession with older men.

They don't notice me watching, of course. No one ever does. I picture her with pink furry handcuffs holding her hands taut against the small of her back as she kneels in front of his hard cock. He pinches her nipples and then allows her to lick the slick, flared tip. The visions in my head leave me wet and throbbing.

I hope I don't leave a damp spot on the back of my skirt. It won't be long, and I will have to take care of myself. Once the crowd thins out a little, that is.

A young couple takes the table to my left. Thrift-store hipsters, they kiss in between sips of their organic soy latte. Holding hands so tightly, as if each is afraid the other will dart off. Both of them are attractive, although slightly cliché and boring, but in my fantasy, they are quite the opposite.

Young college couple, sucking face. He secretly wants to add another boy to the mix; she dreams of tying him up and shoving an organic carrot up his tender, virgin ass. What kind of sex do vegans have? I always imagine it has vegetables involved somehow. No offense to you veggie lovers out there. Or perhaps I've just given you ideas. I fucked myself with a cucumber once, right in the stockroom of the grocery store. Then I put it back in the bin and laughed as I walked away.

I snicker to myself. The vegan couple rub noses. Gag. I am not as turned on as I was a few minutes ago, and instead turn my attention back to the May/December romance at the center table. He is looking at her with a mixture of disdain and lust.

With his right hand, he twists his wedding band as they talk softly. She puts her hand on top of his, but he jerks away from her touch and shakes his head slightly. She bites her lip. I want to stand over her and slap her face.

Young woman sitting with older man has read a certain trilogy too many times. She needs to grow a backbone, then find herself a young blue-collar type, one who will give her the honest, solid fucking that she's really craving. Why do women get involved with married men? It's like they're setting them-selves up for failure. Wait! She looks pissed. She just pushed her chair back and stood up. Wow! She dumped her coffee in his lap and stormed off! Good for you, Blondie!

I snicker, and he glares at me as he dabs at his crotch with a wad of paper napkins. I shrug and hunker over my laptop. The soggy businessman hurries off, and another female employee rushes over to clean up the mess.

"Did you see that? They've been coming in here for the last few weeks; I don't know what she saw in him anyway."

"He probably has a nice-sized bank account." I hate the way my voice sounds, always so small and mousy.

"You got that right. Little Blondie was a gold digger. You need a refill?"

"No thanks." She gives me a smile and a nod and then heads back behind the counter. She's cute, with a ponytail and Keds on her feet. I imagine her swapping hot kisses with red fingernail girl.

I wonder if the two coffee shop girls ever feel each other up in the back room between customers. I'd like to watch them. Small perky tits, henna tattoos; they would be sweet to each other. Maybe one would drizzle caramel topping over the other's nipples, then slowly lick it off while fingers explore wet folds.

I wiggle in my chair, extremely hot and bothered. My eyes

sweep the shop. There is one customer in line and another at a table with his back to me. It's time. I contemplate how to do it. My long, gauzy skirt has pockets. I cut a hole in one of them, to allow for easy access to my pussy. All I have to do is slip my hand in my pocket and finger myself to climax.

However, I'm feeling extra naughty today. With tense fingers, I tease up the hem of my skirt, then stroke my swollen nub. Right there in the middle of the coffee shop. If someone dropped a quarter, and bent down, he could quite possibly catch a glimpse of my wet clit getting a nice massage. It doesn't take me long to reach orgasm. The sweet sensation ripples through my body and makes me gasp just a little, under my breath. Once finished, I pull my skirt back down, lick my finger and resume typing.

Oh, that felt so good. My clit was so hard, like a tiny penis. I yanked up my skirt this time, laying my pussy bare for all the world to see. I fingered it quick, and almost made too much noise when I came. No one is the wiser as I sit here and smolder.

I drink my coffee and remember the first time I masturbated in public. It was six months ago. The therapist I am seeing for my social anxiety disorder advised me to get out in public more, instead of barricading myself in my dorm. I decided the library was a good compromise. It's crowded, but still quiet, a cocoon of friendly books and comfortable chairs.

I found myself an isolated corner and began to read a historical romance novel. The prose was clean and virginal, so I filled in the dirty parts in my head. After a few wild fantasies, I became completely aroused, and decided to head home to the privacy of my dorm for a bit of self-love. A sudden rainstorm prevented me from taking the long walk home, so I scanned the library.

I found the perfect spot: it was secluded, yet still in the open. Anyone could have stumbled upon me, skirt yanked up, fingers inside my panties as I brought myself to a toe-curling orgasm. It was a life-changing experience, so thrilling and naughty. I was hooked from that moment. Suddenly, public places are not so terrifying. Instead, they are opportunities to bask in my new obsession.

Sometimes I fantasize about taking things too far, just to see what would happen. Like maybe I will sit on top of the coffee shop table, pull my skirt up to my waist and spread my legs wide. I will rub my clit with the bowl of one of those little plastic spoons until I scream in mad pleasure. Can you imagine the look on the customers' faces?

I consider leaving, but I'm not quite satisfied. A few new customers have entered the shop. One is a burly construction worker. His faded jeans are tight, showing off a taut, muscular ass. I wonder what his chiseled male perfection would feel like under my hands.

As much as I obsess about sex, I've never performed the act with another. Only myself. More and more lately, I want to experience it. The heat of exchange, tongue kisses, hungry fingers, skin on skin. My disorder prevents me from moving forward. Still, I am close. The burly male sits at the table across from me. He's reading something on his phone as he sips his coffee.

Once again, I publish my thoughts.

Hot construction worker sitting across from me. Black coffee, so honest and unpretentious. His hard body drapes over the chair like he owns it. Black backpack at his feet, his boots heavy and dusty. Dark blond hair curls over his collar, diamond stud in one ear. I wonder if he knows how sexy he is, how he makes my mouth water. The hint of a tattoo peeks out from one tight sleeve.

I stop and take a sip of my mocha, which is now ice cold, then hit the enter key. My words appear as if by magic. Twelve point Times New Roman. Black. My fantasy begins anew, but this time with a twist as I weave myself into the story.

His shoulders are so broad. The skin on his handsome face is bronzed from working outside. Rough fingers. I can almost feel them on my skin. We will meet in a quiet alley. He'll kiss me as he pulls up my skirt. Those rough hands will grip my ass tightly as his tongue explores my mouth. I will lift up one leg, and rest it on his hip, opening myself up for exploration. First, his fingers will slide over my dripping slit. Once wet, they will slide back, and his index finger will push against my puckered hole. It will make me feel like the dirty little slut I really am.

I am starting to sweat as my fingers tap against the keys. He glances in my direction and smiles.

"You're working really hard over there."

"Writing a paper for school." I squeak. Mischievous Mindy is really Mousy Maggie.

"College?"

"Yes."

My foot taps nervously. I want the floor to open up beneath me and swallow me up. It's not that I don't want to talk to him; I do. It's just that the anxiety has me in a choke hold. He is so attractive. In my head I straddle his lap and rub my pussy against his knee until I erupt. In reality, I can barely look him in the eye. There is Xanax in my backpack, a life preserver for when the anxiety threatens to drown me. Knowing the tiny bottle is there comforts me.

"Freshman?"

"Yes. Literature major." Already I have divulged more about myself than usual.

"Going to be a writer, huh? Good for you."

He takes a sip. I love the way his dusky lips caress the edge of the cup as he drinks. His fingers are thick. In my mind, I lie across his lap and let him pull up my skirt. He smacks my bare bottom lightly, just enough to leave a tingle. So much want inside, it consumes me. He looks into his paper cup.

"I need a refill. You?"

"Oh, no thanks."

I watch him as he heads back to the counter, phone in hand, reading voraciously. My fingers find the keys.

If only I had the courage to ask for what I really want. His cock is probably glorious. Thick and hearty, it would spread me open so deliciously wide.

He actually comes back, just as I make the last of my words public, and turns his chair to face mine before his sits down. He stops reading and rewards me with a brilliant grin.

"What's your name, cutie?"

"Maggie." My tongue is thick, and I can barely speak. Can he feel my lust? Will he act on it?

"Ben." He looks at me over his cup as he takes a sip. I notice his deep-brown eyes as they rove over my breasts. I'm wearing a tight light-blue T-shirt, no bra. I like the way he's looking at me, like a hungry wolf eyes a tender lamb. He leans forward slightly. "Where do you go to school?"

"Western University."

"I should have known. The campus is right downtown."

His voice is deep and sensuous. It makes me squirm in my chair. A tiny bit of chest hair is visible at the neck of his T-shirt. I wonder what it would feel like to be wrapped up in those muscular arms while getting fucked by his hard cock. I need to know. The desperation of my lust-filled wanting takes over. Deep inside my brain, something snaps, and a floodgate opens. My mouth forms words, almost on its own.

"Do you start work anytime soon?" I feel my nipples harden and poke at my shirt.

He glances at his watch. "Look at that, I have an hour to

kill." He notices my nipples, and a sly smile forms on his lips.

I smile back. Then close my laptop. I imagine my desire is a brave warrior that slays my fear and frees me from its icy shackles. It's time. I stand up and motion for him to follow. He does, without question. The shop is deserted, save for the two coffee shop girls. They are standing close, whispering to each other as they giggle. We head into the unisex bathroom, and he locks the door behind us.

Before I can blink, our lips meet and we begin to devour each other with mad hunger. Ben tugs at my T-shirt, then pulls it over my head and tosses it aside. He pulls away from my lips and then yanks my skirt down to my ankles. I step out of it and kick it to the side. Now I am naked, save for my sandals. Standing there before him, exposed and vulnerable, causes a delicious thrill to trickle over my body. The deep-brown eyes take in every inch of me, and he smiles, then licks his lips. He pulls me close and takes one of my nipples in his mouth. First he sucks it gently, then grazes it with his teeth. An ember of smoldering heat seems to make a path from the tip of my breast, right down to my clit. I can feel it swell while wetness drips down my inner thighs.

He returns to my mouth and licks my bottom lip while he cups my ass. I mewl like a kitten. My fantasy is coming to life. I lift my right leg and rest my knee against his hip. I feel my pussy spread open for him, slick and juicy. His hand reaches between my legs, and his fingers begin to slide over my wet folds.

"You're so wet, it's dripping all over," he whispers. His index finger slides inside my pussy, then retreats, only to press against my puckered hole. I suck in air over the dirty sensation as Ben's finger slides slowly inside my ass. I feel my muscles squeeze against the intrusion, which only adds to the sinful pleasure.

Ben drops to his knees, keeping his finger inside my ass as he does. His hot tongue laps at my swollen clit. I lean back against the sink to allow him better access. His lips suck the hard knot, while his thumb pushes inside my pussy. The wicked delight of having both holes teased at once threatens to melt me from the inside out. His fingers dive in and out while his lips return to my clit. He sucks and licks until I am clenching in blissful release, pleasure like I have never known.

The orgasm hits me like a tidal wave and drowns me. Panting, I push his head away. The fingers slide out and he stands before me, the tip of his hard cock sticking out of the waistband of his jeans. Wordlessly, I too drop to my knees. The tiled floor is frigid under my skin, in sharp contrast to the fire that is licking my body. I can't get his pants unzipped fast enough. His erect cock is like a steel pipe under my fingers and even more glorious than I imagined.

First, I lick the flared tip, lapping up the pearl of liquid that hangs from it. Bitter heat floods my mouth, while his gentle fingers twist into my hair. He emits a soft moan. It's so much better than my wildest fantasies, flesh and blood throbbing beneath my lips; his musky male scent intoxicates my senses. My virgin mouth continues to suck as I explore his body. I slide my fingers back and stroke him behind his scrotum. The skin feels like velvet under my fingers. I knead his balls next and then take one into my mouth. It causes Ben to arch his back and cry out.

"That's so fucking good."

Hearing his lust puts me over the edge. I continue to lavish attention on his scrotum while I use my free hand to finger my clit. In seconds I am dropping headfirst into ecstasy as my body shudders in yet another powerful orgasm. Ben gasps as I take his cock behind my lips and suck him in deeper.

"I'm going to…"

He tightens, and I feel a vibration in his scrotum. I do not pull away; instead, I drink in his essence. The salty tang burns my throat as I swallow, yet I welcome the sensation. Never have I felt more alive than at this moment. I lick the head, taking every drop he has to offer. Ben pulls me to my feet and gives my ass a gentle slap.

"I hope you enjoyed that as much as I did, Mischievous Mindy."

I HATE SEX

Tamsin Flowers

I hate sex. There, I've said it out loud. I know, in this world, that makes me some kind of freak but, with billions of people on the planet, there are bound to be a few of us who just don't get it. The mess and the intimacy.

I hate sex and I work in a sex shop. I can see that puzzles you. No, it really doesn't make sense for someone who hates sex to work in a sex shop. But the job ad simply said retail experience required, and I've got plenty of that. I was laid off when my last place closed down, I needed work and so I answered the ad.

Of course, I didn't mention during my interview how much I hate sex. Or admit the fact that I hadn't had sex in, let me see, going on five years. No, when I went to meet with Archie Bennett, the oleaginous owner of Silicone Dreams—sex emporium for the discerning—I dazzled him with my resume. Years spent in big department stores and upmarket boutiques. If anyone knows anything about selling on the shop floor, it's me.

And that's what Archie employs me to do, not to have sex with the customers.

Naturally, you might think that working in a sex shop would gradually thaw my *froidure* but, no, it hasn't. I've been working here for six months now and I still hate sex just as much. Possibly even more. After all, if it's sex all day at work, so to speak, it's the last thing you're interested in when you get home at night. A delicious meal, a glass of wine, my feet up on the coffee table as I relax on the couch with a good book or a great movie...that's what works for me. Not humping some sweaty idiot whose name I can't remember.

But don't think for one minute that my distaste for the act itself detracts from my ability to peddle sexual accoutrements. I can advise you in minute detail which strap-on would be right for you and your loved one; I can run through the relative merits and functional variants of the sixty-three vibrators we hold in stock; or if you tell me a bit about your girl, I'll tell you which condom to pick. Just don't expect me to measure you up for a butt plug.

So I hate sex—but I don't hate my work. Actually, I quite enjoy working at Silicone Dreams. It's a little less formal than Macy's, a little less up its own ass than some of the boutiques I've worked in and the customers are more colorful. I have three coworkers: oily boss-man Archie and the other two salesgirls, Alexa and Honey. We get on, we have a laugh even with Archie and, though the pay's not great, I've worked in far worse places.

It would be safe to say that both Honey and Alexa do enjoy sex—in a big way. They enjoy doing it, they enjoy talking about it and of course they enjoy their work. They flirt with the customers more than I do or, should I say, they enjoy it more than I do. We all do it; flirting with the customers is the best way to make sales and we're working on commission. Honey makes the most money. Long blonde hair, serious curves and wide blue eyes that make her look like an innocent schoolgirl, even though she's pushing twenty-five. She has her own little fan club, a bunch of men who come into the store when they know she'll be working and buzz around her for hours. She humors them, they spend money and Archie's happy.

Fly Guy is her biggest fan. Honey works five days a week and you can set your watch by the fact that Fly Guy will come in, just after lunch, on at least four of those days. He's smooth, slick, in his midthirties with the looks of a male model gone to seed. Just a little softening of the jowls, a small overhang of belly nudging at the top of his Levi's. Shirt undone one button too low. One spritz too many of a cologne he should have spent more money on. But his eyes light up when he walks into the store and sees us standing behind the counter, Honey always ready to show him the newest stock or plug the merits of an old favorite. He's a little shy but he's polite, which is more than can be said for some of the guys that come in here.

When he's gone, I tease Honey.

"Fly Guy's gonna ask you out. He's just working up the nerve. Next time, I'd put ten on it."

Honey laughs her throaty, sexy laugh but she'll never take the bet. I wonder if she'll say yes or no when it finally happens.

It's a rule that there are always two of us girls working in the shop together in case of weirdos. Which we get plenty of. Most of them are friendly and harmless, but there have been incidents. So now we always work in pairs. Usually Archie's up in his office above the shop, and I happen to know he's keeps a piece in one of his desk drawers. So weirdos, beware.

But Honey's blue eyes and winsome smile have made her a little spoilt. She's used to getting what she wants, and she can be a bitch if she doesn't. So every now and then, when she's in the hot throes of a new passion, she sneaks off, mid-shift, for a little afternoon delight in the back of her boyfriend's car on some parking lot around the corner. She's never gone long; it doesn't take Honey more than fifteen or twenty minutes to get her guy's rocks off and her own. Then she's back, breathless and smiling, full of charm for the rest of the afternoon.

Tuesday afternoons are always quiet and, on this particular Tuesday, Honey was out on one of her little field trips. I was alone in the store and there hadn't been any customers for some time. It probably wouldn't pick up again until the after-work rush. I was propping up the counter, processing customer orders; you'd be surprised at some of our best-selling items.

The bell jangled and I heard the door swing open. I looked up to see Fly Guy coming in. He walked straight up to the counter.

"Honey's not here," I said.

"I know. I saw her leaving a few minutes ago."

"She'll be back in twenty minutes," I said, wondering why he had come into the shop if he knew Honey wasn't here.

"I know," he said.

He was leaning slightly forward with his palms flat on the counter. His eyes held mine without blinking.

"How do you know?" This was weird.

"I saw her hooking up with a guy on the corner. And twenty minutes, that's how long it probably takes."

His cologne was invading my nostrils, and I took a deep breath of it.

"Your name's Melba, isn't it?"

I nodded. I knew his name was Charlie but he'd been Fly Guy for so long that Charlie didn't seem right.

"How can I help you?" I said, and I really was wondering what he wanted.

"Honey said you'd be getting a new range of fingertip vibes in this week," he said. "Have they arrived yet?"

The shelf where we display the vibrating toys is right at the back of the store and can't be seen from the door. He followed me around a display unit of peekaboo bras and crotchless panties and down the aisle to where the new range had just been put out on display.

"They're here," I said, indicating them with my hand.

He barely glanced at them. Instead his eyes were riveted on mine and in the narrow confines of the aisle I could feel heat radiating from his body. I wanted to go back to the counter where the glass top could act as a barrier between us, but I felt paralyzed by his scrutiny.

"If you want to wait for Honey…"

"No." He cleared his throat. "I came here to see you, Melba."

I didn't know what to say. I didn't move away but I didn't move any closer to him. Deep inside me there was the pang of an echo going off; like the sonar bleep in a submarine; something long remembered, half forgotten, was registering its presence low in my abdomen. I didn't want to feel this way. Fly Guy, Charlie, whoever he was—I hardly knew him. I hadn't thought of him like this. Shit! I hadn't thought of anyone like this for an age.

He wasn't in any hurry. He stood in front of the rack of electronic sex toys, waiting for me to be ready. He didn't say a word, he hardly blinked and his breathing remained calm and even. I felt the opposite. My heart was racing, and I was astonished by the way my body was reacting to him. Despite the air-conditioning, between the tall shelving units and the back of the store the air was hot and dry. Oxygen depleted. I breathed deeper but I felt light-headed. A prickling sensation crept across my belly and up my back. I think the hairs on my arm were standing up.

As I became overwhelmed by the unfamiliar play of desire through my body, he stood stock still, waiting for me.

I didn't know what to do. I tore my eyes from his to look down at his groin. My hand twitched, a treacherous betrayal. I bit my lip and looked away, suffused with the feeling that I was about to cry. He said nothing, did nothing, and I was losing control. Admitting to myself that I wanted him so goddamned badly was tearing me apart. I don't like sex, I don't want sex, I don't do sex. That was my mantra. Then Fly Guy walks in, puts me in a confined space and there's only one thing I can think of.

A sigh, almost a whimper, escaped my lips.

"You're ready."

Finally he made a move. He reached over to the shelf opposite and helped himself to a pair of red leather cuffs.

"Your hands," he said.

I held up my hands to him, wrists uppermost, the gesture of the supplicant. He knew what I needed, and my heart thundered in my chest as I realized he was going to give it to me. He attached the cuffs and spun me around so that I was facing the shelving unit. Within moments my hands were secured above my head. I couldn't see what he was doing, only hear him taking items from the shelves around us.

I suddenly panicked and struggled against the cuffs. But I wasn't really afraid of him; I was fighting against my own feelings of shame. Part of me wanted what was going to happen next. Part of me didn't. And the wanting part shocked me.

Fly Guy stroked my back to calm me in the same way a groom would handle a skittish horse.

"We don't have long," he whispered in my ear.

But he took care to be gentle as he pushed my skirt up over

my hips. I was wet already but when he skimmed a finger along the side of my damp panties, I felt a buildup of heat and pressure deep inside my pussy. And as his finger pushed its way between my lips, a gush, a flood, years of pent-up frustration broke free. I moaned. I wanted this so badly and at the same time I didn't want it at all. I didn't know what I wanted.

But my hips knew. They writhed under his touch. And my legs knew. When he pulled my panties down to my ankles, my legs stepped out of them and spread themselves wide. My breasts knew, pebbling up and pushing against the constraint of my bra. My skin knew, every inch of it straining for the stroke of his hand. I cried when he touched my ass, it felt so good. So wholly unexpected and unfamiliar. A firm, warm hand on a place that had forgotten the feeling of human skin sliding across human skin.

I heard the rasp of his zipper and the ripping of condom foil. Then came the delicious rubbery smell and the rustle of the condom being unfurled, but I could hardly stand the wait. It was the thing I thought I wanted least in the world and now all of a sudden I wanted more than anything. The tip of his cock nudged against my dripping labia, while one of his fingers opened up a path for it. I pushed my hips back to meet it, and it slid inside more easily than I had a right to expect. But its arrival reinstated a surge of sensations through my body that I'd long ago banished from my mind and fought hard to forget: pulsing, throbbing, rippling. I caught my breath and bit my tongue, adding a salty metallic tang to a mouth that was already watering.

Charlie brought his hands around to the front of me and pushed my bra up until my breasts flopped free. He pinched my nipples as he pumped into me from behind, dissolving me. My mouth was dry and if I hadn't been able to grasp the shelf my wrists were strapped to, my legs certainly wouldn't have been able to carry my weight. He pushed in and out of me fast and hard, making no sound apart from the rasping of his breath at my shoulder.

I felt my climax riding in from a long way off, appearing on the horizon and looming larger as it came closer. My back arched against his chest and he dropped one of his hands down to work my clit, that poor, lonely nub that had been so neglected for so long. And, oh, this man knew what he was doing; he knew how to push the button. He was never going to need a fingertip vibe. An orgasm, my first in ages, exploded inside me, ripping through me, bursting over me…piercing and sudden. I gasped but it came out louder than a gasp. I didn't care; I'd forgotten where I was, even who I was with. I was simply riding out the pleasure as my body took what I'd been denying it for so long, every nerve and muscle fiber telling me I'd been wrong about how much I hated it.

Charlie grasped me tight against him as he pushed deeper still. A small grunt and his rigid hips told me he was coming too. As he pulled out of me, I heard a footfall on the staircase above.

Fuck!

"Everything okay down there, girls?"

It was Archie. He must have heard something. Not something. Me.

"We're all good," I called out, as Fly Guy quickly undid the cuffs on my wrists and released me from the shelving unit.

I adjusted my bra and tucked my blouse into my skirt. Then I looked around the floor for my panties. But Fly Guy beat me to it. He picked up the scrap of pink silk and, looking me straight in the eye, slipped them into his pocket.

"Will you come back?" I said.

"No," he said with a shrug. "There are too many girls like

you in this city who need my help. But you'll find someone else who can do it to you just as good."

Fly Guy and his ego. Healer of the frigid, smelter of the ice queens.

As he left the store at the front, Honey came in through the back looking as pink and flushed as I probably was.

"Was that Fly Guy I just missed?" she said.

I nodded.

"He'll be back," she said, checking her hair in the mirror behind the counter.

I said nothing.

I should start this story over.

I love sex. I work in a sex shop and I love sex....

TOYS

Jade A. Waters

Jennifer thought her toy collection was a little excessive, but she couldn't help herself.

She'd amassed a bounty of equipment: dildos, vibrators, cuffs, whips, plugs, beads and various other oddities—like the specialty pair of vibrating electric nipple clamps she'd stumbled upon on her last vacation out of the country—and all of them had added to her secretly adored stash. The dildos came in numerous shapes and sizes, ranging from the foot-long Black Rock to the tiny purple Tipper. And the vibrators—well, Jennifer took great pride in those, each of them appropriate in different scenarios, depending on the strength of the vibe she needed.

Originally, her stash fit under some panties in a special closet drawer. Soon, though, it grew, because it seemed the longer she'd been away from sex, the hungrier she got for more toys. Buying them kept her warm and aching for more, and her collection now filled a small moving box in the back of her closet.

A four-by-four-foot one, to be precise.

So, when Daniel rolled off Jennifer after their twelfth fuck—
and she, again, hadn't come—she cast a frustrated glance at her
closet while she worried that maybe she'd ruined herself with
the toys.

"Did you?" Daniel panted, resting one hand on her stomach
and the other on his withered shaft. He peered at her with a
hopeful grin, and Jennifer felt a new burn of color washing
aside the flush she'd earned from hours of fucking her new
boyfriend.

"Well," she said, "not exactly."

"Damn." Daniel wedged himself against her. He was everything she sought in a bed buddy: his scent was pleasant, his eyes
were warm and his swimmer's body had made her panties wet
the second she'd noticed the hip bones showing over his trunks.
He was so delightful she mentally kicked herself for the hours of
howling orgasms she couldn't seem to have.

"Yeah. Kind of weird," she muttered. Jennifer pressed her
lips on his—damn, he could kiss—but her body throbbed with
hornier aspirations.

"Tell me what to do." Daniel slipped his arm beneath her so
he could wrap her in a hug, then grazed her neck with his lips.
"I want you to be having as much fun as I am—"

"Oh, I'm having fun. I'm just not…there."

She wanted to scream.

"Well, let's get you there." Daniel squeezed her tighter. "I
really like you, Jennifer. I'm officially denying myself any more
orgasms until you have one."

She laughed. His sense of humor, paired with his incredibly
sweet nature, had been the second thing to wet her panties after
she met him, which is why they'd started dating shortly there-
after and screwing around a few weeks after that.

But now they'd been screwing for a month, and while she

knew Daniel was extremely patient, she also knew he wanted her to come. It wasn't a pride thing for him—just a good, caring man thing. She was his girl. He was her man.

And he wanted to please her, about which she certainly had no complaints.

"Seriously, darling. Anything. Tell me what I can do to make this happen for you." He kissed her again. "Anything. Do you want me to put on a costume? Dance around? Strip for you?" He gulped. "Do you want to stick something in weird places?"

Jennifer couldn't stop the laughter that poured out of her mouth, but when Daniel rolled over her again and pushed his semierect length against her, she stopped abruptly.

"Anything," he repeated. "Tell me."

"Okay." Jennifer took a breath. Real men could handle toys. The few who had run off when they spied her collection—way back when it was not even half the size it was now—simply weren't real men.

Right?

"I really hope this doesn't freak you out."

"Anything," he whispered. He rubbed against her and Jennifer moaned.

"There's a box of...toys...in my closet."

"Oh?"

She stared into his face, waiting to see his panic. His disgust. His disdain. His horror.

But there was none.

"And you didn't tell me about this before because...?"

"There are a lot of them," she blurted. "I think it might be intimidating."

Daniel tucked his pelvis to make firm contact with her again, making her keenly aware of the warmth of her pussy. She wanted to just take him in, to feel him riding her passionately all over again while she crossed her fingers and hoped for the best—but the truth was that she knew they'd need a hand at this point. Her brain was on overload, and thoughts of him using the toys to manipulate her were putting her right on the edge. She chewed her lip and Daniel shook his head.

"I'm not going to be intimidated. As long as I get to touch you, I'm not frightened by a few little toys."

She sighed. They weren't little, and there definitely weren't a few.

"Okay," she said. Her voice sounded meek in her ears. Would he really be okay with this? "Only if you're sure."

Daniel dropped his lips to her chest and ran his tongue over her nipples. She shivered as they stiffened against his mouth, both of them raw from his earlier tweaks and kisses. When she gasped, he dragged his mouth over her collarbone before pulling back to grin. "Are you kidding? I said anything to make you come, beautiful."

And then he was up by her closet, poking around for the giant box of embarrassing things that she'd been hiding from most of the men she'd screwed in the last five years.

"Is this it?" He tugged the box out from behind her mountain of shoes and then dropped it on the carpet beside the bed. Rubbing his forehead, he settled his hands on his hips. "Um, wow. This is somewhat impressive."

Jennifer buried her face in the pillow. "I'm so embarrassed."

"Don't be." Daniel ignored the box to kneel beside the bed. He tickled her side until she peeked up. "Jennifer, I want you to feel good too. I told you I like you. Now, before I open this…" he glanced back at the box, "very large collection of things that will make you feel better, do you have a preference? Anything you'd like me to use?"

She rotated her head enough to expose one eye. He looked

sincere, and his hand caressing the arch of her back didn't hurt either. She muttered, "Surprise me." Then her heart cranked in her chest. Had she really found a man who was as game for toys as she was? "Honestly, I'm excited to see what you pick."

Daniel lowered himself to a sitting position. His eyes widened as he opened the flaps of the box, and Jennifer held back a laugh as he withdrew toy after toy from inside.

The Rabbit.

The fuzzy cuffs.

The ben-wa balls.

The blue-glitter butt plug.

"Have you used all of these?" he asked, his voice serious as he lowered a shiny ceramic dildo to the carpet. This one he fondled before reaching back in.

"No." She scooted to the edge of the bed, grabbing a flap of the box so she could see him rummaging through. He didn't seem deterred, giving each item careful consideration as he laid them out on the floor, and as he arranged them in a neat row she grew even more excited. He removed the Black Rock, waving it around in the air with a raise of his eyebrows, and tingles ricocheted through her body. "I've used a lot of them, but mostly I've discovered I like collecting them."

Daniel grasped the nipple clamps with both hands and splayed them in front of his face. "These?" he asked, tilting his head.

"Never used."

He gave the rest of the contents a peek over. Then he looked to her, and something in his gaze made her tremble.

"I have an idea." He crawled over to the bed, planting his lips on hers before running his hand down her belly and between her thighs. He teased her with a quick exploration of her outer folds, and Jennifer moaned when he yanked his hand away. "Close your eyes and I'll pick something." He paused to slip his tongue into her mouth, twirling it in a more frenzied movement than usual. Suddenly, he stopped.

"And then, I'm going to fuck you until you cry out for me, over and over again. What do you think?"

Jennifer gasped. "Oh wow. Yes, please." She closed her eyes as directed, feeling the shifts of the bed as Daniel climbed back down to the floor. The anticipation was more intense with her eyes shut, the room's air tickling her pert nipples and the abandoned, heated creases of her sex. She tried to stay calm as she listened to the sounds of him riffling through the box.

"Oh yes. This is it."

What had he grabbed?

"Keep your eyes closed, okay?"

"Yes." He crawled over her and settled his weight on her thighs. She could feel his gaze over her, and his fully hardened cock now nudged her about an inch below her pussy.

Daniel laid his hand over her mound. He circled his fingers over her trimmed curls, and then dipped one of them between her folds to graze her opening. "Jennifer...you're soaked already." He grunted in approval. "I can't wait to see what happens when I use your toy on you."

Jennifer squirmed.

Was it a vibrator?

Had he chosen a dildo?

"Or maybe toys."

Her inner walls tightened. *A plug?*

Daniel shoved his finger into her and she moaned. "Dammit, baby, you're so wet I could fuck you right now, but I won't. None for me until you come." He rolled off and licked her belly, tracing his tongue down until he lingered above her clit, and Jennifer pinched her eyes shut tighter. She already wanted to scream, and the slow glides of his finger while he blew hot air against her mound made for the sweetest torture.

"Please," she whispered.

But Daniel withdrew his finger.

Before she could speak, he pressed the silicone head of one of her dildos against her. Jennifer wasn't sure which one it was, and she inhaled while Daniel adjusted the tip to fit inside her opening.

"Do you like that?"

She nodded. He inched it farther, moving so slowly the thick plastic rubbed along her walls in the most delightful of ways. Once the base struck her folds, Daniel jerked it back until only the tip remained inside her.

Jennifer growled at the immediate emptiness. "More," she begged.

Daniel obliged, repeating his movement a few times. Each time he glided the silicone rod so that it banged hard against her depths, then drew it almost all the way out. Jennifer's face grew numb, and when her breath became ragged, Daniel released a moan.

"I'm enjoying getting to watch how you quiver when I fuck you with this," he said. "I wish you could see how lovely you are. Your breasts are so full, and your belly practically heaves with your breath. You know your thighs are shaking?"

Yes indeed, she did.

He jammed the dildo inside her again, this time leaving it planted.

"I want to feel you," she whispered. She loved her toys, and they'd gotten her through all this time away from human contact—but she wanted Daniel inside of her now. He had to be a part of this.

"You will," he said.

Then he turned on one of her vibrators.

Jennifer clenched around the dildo as he pressed the vibrator against her swollen bud, using his other hand to wedge the other toy inside her. She moaned and shoved herself down, loving the combination she'd tried so many times on her own. Daniel had picked her favorite vibe, too—the one that went from low to high with an easy flick of the wrist, its special jelly tip practically molding to the shape of her clit. He rubbed it over her, then began sliding the dildo in and back out. She wanted him in its stead, but deep inside, her orgasm built—the thundering presence held back despite all of Daniel's moves, sweet words and caresses.

"How does that feel, baby?"

She could tell he'd propped himself on his knees to balance, the bed wobbling as he worked the dildo inside her and wiggled his wrist so the vibrator directly tickled her clit. She heard the crinkle of a wrapper and she trembled, aching to feel him.

"Oh god it feels so good. Please, please," she said, gritting her teeth. "Fuck me, Daniel."

"Open your eyes," he said.

She did. Daniel hovered over her, the muscles of his arms flexing as he pumped the dildo and whisked over her swollen bead with the vibrator. He bit his lip as he manipulated her, his wrapped cock now at full attention a few inches from her thigh.

"Please," she whispered.

He drew the dildo from her pussy, the rubber slick with her wetness. He tossed it aside but kept the vibe against her clit, flicking it back and forth and sliding his length closer to her opening. She writhed to meet him and Daniel continued to tease, taking light grazes with his crown to make her whimper. Jennifer clawed at his sides, trying to urge him forward, and he folded over her for a heavy kiss before positioning himself square with her cunt.

"Ready?" he said.

"Yes!"

Daniel thrust then, so firm in comparison to the dildo. He sank far deeper than the plastic rod, his girth magnificent and filling, and drawing a loud cry from her lips. He grunted and pounded into her, continuing to rub the vibrator over her clit. The orgasm that had teased her for so long snuck closer, warning her of its onslaught in a spray of goose bumps that lined her arms and legs. Deep inside, she felt that spark—exactly where he touched and probed, working her into a frenzy that made her arch to meet him.

"You feel so good!" Jennifer gasped.

Daniel plundered her mouth with another kiss and then sucked in a breath as he drove into her again. "I'm still not coming. Not yet. You first." He plunged again, hard, and Jennifer threw her head back as the sensation took over, a rolling crescendo that made her scream.

"Yes!" Her thighs shook as he pressed into her and Jennifer could no longer see or hear, her mind filling with the intensity that Daniel's eager thrusts brought to her. She groaned and bucked against him, and he swiped the vibrator faster against her clit until she cried, "Oh god yes, yes, yes!"

When she jerked, Daniel countered her in a skillful ride, his free hand gripping her hips and then her breasts. Jennifer's orgasm came overwhelming and sweet, ripping through her like a tornado and making her moan so loud she thought she'd deafened herself. As she settled into the feeling, all the worries she'd had washed away until she lay panting beneath him.

Daniel slowed, and then lodged himself as deep as he could go while her muscles still spasmed around him. He hadn't moved the vibrator, and as it kept right on buzzing over her clit, he stared down at her with a beaming smile.

"You are fucking hot," he said.

She giggled. "So are you."

He shifted inside her and she jumped. "I'm not done with you, though."

"No?" Jennifer put her hands over her cheeks, both of them hot and tingling from the solid minute she'd stopped breathing. The vibrator against her clit still felt so good, as did Daniel's throbbing cock inside her.

"Definitely not." He eased out and slid roughly in, panting as he tried to hold back. When he rubbed her with the vibrator again, she felt her second climax take root, coming out of nowhere and making her cry as she shoved herself up to meet him. Daniel lost his control then, biting her shoulder as he sped his pace inside her.

"Jennifer…" he moaned, and as he drove forward she shuddered, the wave of pleasure hardly giving her time to breathe.

"Oh, Daniel!"

He groaned and rode her excitement. Jennifer clawed her hands down his sides, feeling the vibration from the toy all the way into her core as he slammed, retreated and forced himself inside of her again. Finally he filled her with one loud moan and Jennifer sighed with the movement, her body completely weak. Daniel fell over her and buried his lips in her hair.

"Wow." Between them, the vibrator continued to buzz. It had rolled slightly off to the side at an angle that rubbed against both of their hips. A grin spread over Jennifer's face as she realized what had happened.

"That was amazing," she said.

Daniel lifted himself, his face red and his breathing still precarious. He kissed her mouth, her cheeks and then her forehead. Slowly he drew himself away, and a pout touched her lips.

"Yes, it was," he said. He turned off the vibrator, then held it in front of her. "This, all of it, was beautiful. I am hooked."

They lay still for a few minutes, Daniel resting the vibrator on her chest as he stared into her eyes. When they calmed, he picked it up again and tapped it against her sternum.

"You know, I'm not sure about the rest of the contents of the box."

"What do you mean?"

Daniel ran the vibrator in small circles down her belly until it rested against her opening. "I mean," he said, smiling, "I'm not sure how they all work for you."

Jennifer gasped.

"Guess we better start working through the rest of the box."

HER FOREST, HER RULES

Laila Blake

Her heart hammering faster than the distant drums, Amy ducked under a low branch and then caught herself against a tree. The bark was rough under her short, pink fingers. Carefully, she peered around the trunk, daring a glance back. Trees, moss, roots, grass—but not another soul. She could still hear them, trampling around in the distance. There were shouts; someone was blowing a horn but she didn't have anybody directly on her tail. This did not come as a great surprise to her, really, but there was little fun in not even pretending.

Finally, she pushed herself off the tree. She had to get deeper into the forest if she wanted to keep her edge. Maybe there were allies to be found deeper in its mossy glens. She seemed to remember a clearing that had served as a resting place for her clan before.

The underbrush crackled under each step; larger branches creaked like the moan of an ancient spirit, smaller ones simply broke under the impact. Stealth had never been one of Amy's strong suits; just like dashing from cover to cover, a zigzagging line between the trees was far more fluid and elegant in her fantasy then it presented itself to the casual observer watching her.

The deeper she got into the forest and the farther she distanced herself from the trodden paths, the slower her progress. She had to stop more often to catch her breath, had to take more careful steps to avoid tripping, falling or making too much noise. When it felt momentarily as though someone was holding her back, she stopped, whirled around and then slapped her hand over her mouth at the sound of tearing fabric.

"Fuck!" She cursed in an audible whisper, sank onto a fallen tree and lifted the torn hem of her wide velvet skirt up over her knee to inspect it. It was large and ugly and she'd left her stitching kit back at camp. "Fuck-bloody damned…"

Her tirade stopped instantly when she found herself looking up at a sword, its tip gently coming to rest under her chin. Both Amy's eyes and her mouth opened wider. How in the world had he sneaked up on her like that?

"What do we have here…" a warm raspy voice asked mockingly, "a cursing elf? An anachronistically cursing elf, what's more. There are rules against such conduct, wench…."

Amy couldn't answer; every single molecule of air seemed to have vacated her lungs for the present. The sword-wielder was one of the few members of their club who didn't turn up every time. She had seen him before and admired him, but he'd never dropped his role, and she had no idea where he came from or where he went on the weekends he didn't attend. He had beautiful gear that didn't have the unrealistic sheen of brand-new materials to it and sometimes she wondered if he met with other larpers, too.

It was just that he didn't really look like one—at least not like anyone from her club—he wore the leather breastplate like none of the others, boys all of them and whatever armor, wizard's robes or ear extensions they invoked to suspend disbelief, their malleable, soft faces, zits and hair product always got in the way. Amy did not voice those complaints of course—she was on thin ice herself. Who had ever heard of a chubby elf? And really that was the point, that here, one of them had to feel like an outsider, the way she did almost everywhere else.

This one though, he was different. He seemed to be one of the few men in the group who looked their age—they were all in their late twenties and early thirties, but so few looked it, especially among the men. The sword-wielder did, though; his hair was cropped almost as short as the stubble of his beard. He wore an expression of condescension that suited his armor and stance and Amy was momentarily taken aback at how deeply he seemed to be immersed in his role. There was not a hidden grin, not a wink, not a gesture out of place. She could feel a twinge deep between her legs.

"Got a name elf?"

Amy swallowed, then dropped the hem of her skirt back down over her leather shoes and tried to arrange her features into a defiant scowl.

"Who wants to know?" she asked back, fingers gliding over the glued-on prosthetics on her ears that made them nice and pointy. When she saw him noticing, she quickly snapped them back into her lap, where they felt useless.

As though he had guessed this problem, Amy suddenly felt him bring his sword closer. The sharp point was pushing against her skin. Right there under her chin where a tiny amalgamation of fatty tissue made just enough of a curve for him to poke at. The sword was not sharp—but it was real metal and Amy swallowed uncomfortably. Then she raised her hands, yielding.

He hadn't said another word, just cocked up his brow and ignored her back talk. His eyes were locked on hers, and while she found herself blushing, his face showed no sign of discomfort or embarrassment. Just for a moment, Amy could give in to the fantasy that he really was a warrior who had come to capture her. A shiver went down her spine, and she wet her lips.

"Amariel," she finally whispered, voice croaking a little. The sword had a greater effect on her than she was willing to admit to herself. "My name, human, is Amariel. And I would be very much obliged if you could...back the fuck off."

She blushed harder, annoyance glinting in her eyes—more at herself for her inability to stay in character and come up with the right things to say than with the guy, but it was easy to transfer those things. Especially because it seemed to be his eyes and the cocky set of his brows that caused her brain to go to mush.

He smirked and lowered his sword. Amy swallowed; she was about to touch her neck in relief when she felt the tip now resting against her chest, just above the swell of her breasts, bound and squished together by a cheap fake leather corset.

"You know I can't do that," he rasped. The tip of the sword sank lower along her sternum; the metal was cold against her skin and Amy shivered. Her hands started to prickle from holding them up and she bit her lips while he continued: "I have my orders...any elves in our forests are taken in for questioning. But then you know that, don't you? That's why you ran...."

The sword was still scraping along her skin until it rested on the hard top of her corset. The point of the blade was completely submerged between her breasts. Amy quivered and looked up at the man, wide-eyed and momentarily shocked. It wasn't like she had never fantasized about this. Her friend—a skinny enchantress with a costume that even Amy couldn't take her eyes off of—had told her this kind of stuff went on sometimes, but it had never happened to Amy. She licked her bottom lip and breathed in the smell of the forest—wet and alive. She was making this up, surely.

"Well...if you have orders, human..." She tried to sound unimpressed and pointedly looked down at the sword between her pillowing breasts. "I myself have little interest in meeting your captain."

He moved like the wind—that was the last thing she thought before everything happened all too quickly. The sword clattered to the ground and she felt herself bodily pulled off the log, turned and pushed against a nearby tree. The force of impact made her grunt—and then whine when the man pulled back her arm and angled it up on her back, just the way she had seen in a hundred cop movies.

There were two ways to step out of the game. There was a word and a hand signal—and for that reason it was never allowed to incapacitate hands and mouth at the same time. Amy knew them both, the word rolled around in her head and her fingers tightened on the rough bark as she felt that warm shiver run down her spine. She could say the word and he would back off, but then the tingling would stop and so would the throbbing between her legs. Briefly, she considered if this made her slutty— but then the very idea of being exactly that made her heart beat faster. She didn't often have the opportunity to be and now that it seemed right within her grasp, all she wanted was a taste.

"Is that so?" he growled into her ear. He was taller than she was, bending over a little to get close to her dark hair. He brushed it from her neck with his free hand, while the other tightened slightly on her wrist.

"Oh...yes," she exhaled. It came out much more a grunt than her regular voice and she tried to remedy that when she continued, working harder to keep up her role. "I hear that...in humans, you get duller and duller with each...rank you climb."

He pulled her arm up higher, and she moaned and suddenly could feel his groin on her behind. "Terrible conversationalists," she continued in open defiance, even as her ass instinctively pushed back against him. She had spent every first weekend of the last sixteen months in costume, spouting elf lore and feeling geeky even amongst her peers, but here she was—and nothing could have been more exciting.

"Whereas elves are known for their raucous feasting..." the man replied, his voice dripping with sarcasm—and something else. "How well do you know humans, elf?"

"I told you my name, stop calling me elf," she whispered, her voice hoarse against the bark of the tree. She could feel her own hot breath deflected, leaving the slightest trace of moisture on her cheek. "And tell me yours."

"Making demands now, eh?" Amy could hear his smile, then feel a hand in the curve of her waist, strong fingers dragging down with the grain of her velvet dress over the wide curve her hip. "Gohan." A voice like the growl of distant thunder.

"I saw you running this way, elf," he continued. A lip brushed over the shell of ear. "Knew I wanted to be the one to catch you."

Her knees buckled and Amy held on tighter to the tree. Her cheek was resting on bark and she was sure that she could smell the resin in its depths, hear the insects feeding and the birds far above. She felt like an elf then, truly, for the first time.

"And now that you've got me..." she asked voice hoarse and raspy with feeling, "what are planning on doing with me?" She leaned her head back just enough to lay it against his shoulder, to brush her cheek against the stubble of his beard—this was what confident women asked in the movies, how wrong could it be? At the same time, she pushed her rear against his eager hand.

Encouraged, he brushed it down her hip and cupped one round cheek. His hand could not nearly cover it, but it felt like that was exactly what he was doing when his thumb found the crack of her ass all the way through dress and panties and bore down on it. Amy gasped; the corset forced her hard breath to expand her lungs upward rather than outward, causing her breasts to bob up and down with each inhale.

"I had some ideas," he growled, fisting her dress so that it lifted a few inches off her ankles. "But I'm not adverse to some new ones...."

She could feel the wind on her calves. The part of her brain that was still unsure about the whole venture tried to point out that this wasn't her—that she had never acted this brazenly in her entire life. But it wasn't her; that was the point. She was Amariel—and Amariel would have been no stranger to using her body as leverage to escape capture from this human who had a voice that ran through her veins all the way into her chest, like the deep bass of a dance tune.

"The way I see it, human," she said, as he pulled up her skirt higher, inches at a time. "I would much rather spend time with you than your captain." The velvet was starting to bunch on the swell of her ass, just below the bottom of her corset. The wind had reached the sensitive back of her knees and he could reach for the hem now, pulling the rest up in one go. Amy gasped and immediately, his hand was there, warming her flesh, rubbing the rising goose pimples away.

His breath was faster, too, she could feel it in on the side of her neck. This wasn't normal, the voice in her head said. Normal people went out for a date or two. She didn't even have to insist on three but this was insane—anybody could come and see them, anybody! And yet, she didn't move away. His fingers thanked her by finding their way between her thighs and against the moist panel of her panties. They were anachronistic, too.

"Do you consent, elf?" he finally growled, almost panting with the effort of holding himself back. He tugged at her arm again—Amy had almost forgotten he was still keeping her immobile. She whimpered as his hand tightened its grip and then nodded hard.

"Yes…yes," she all but moaned and a moment later, her arm was free. At least it was for a second, before his hands grasped her hips and pulled her back a foot or so. Instinctively, her hands found support against the tree. There was the rustling of material behind her; the leather had such a distinctive sound as he slapped it away. Then his foot found hers, pushing her legs apart with as much roughness as the scene required. He ran his fingers up her shapely thighs and then wormed them under the flexible dark elastic.

"Bad elf," he growled, rubbing along her wet slit, making her gasp and moan. "What insects spin yarn as fine as this?"

"Magic ones," she exhaled and then cried out when he pinched her clit as though in punishment. Red-hot arousal pulsed through the tiny pleasure knob. He pulled the stretch fabric to one side until it rested in the crack of her ass. He squeezed the naked cheek hard enough to make her moan again, and suddenly she felt something else entirely pushing against her exposed folds.

"Like your elf-cunt? Magic?" His teeth were on her shoulder when he pushed inside of her—slow and deep. Amy could have cried it felt so good—after months without sex, she was tight but wet enough for it not to matter. She wanted to reply, tried to take a deep breath, but when she opened her lips to speak she felt his fingers invading her mouth, curling against her tongue. She could taste herself on his skin, wet and salty, and she sucked at the fingers eagerly. For a moment, the forest seemed to spin on his axis and when the feeling of vertigo left her head, she was sucking to the beat of his hard thrusts.

"Touch yourself," he commanded in another groan and however humiliating it would have seemed to her only minutes ago, Amy hastened to pull up the front of her skirt as well and buried her fingers against her clit, rubbing, pulling and falling in rhythm with his thrusts.

"Good elf," he rasped. Stifling her moans was becoming a more and more difficult task. He pushed harder; Amy tried to keep pace, but she could feel by the tightness of his grasp on her hip that he was holding on for dear life. Instinctively, she bore down harder on her clit, coming mere moments later with a gasp of surprise and heady exhaustion.

"Fuck," he shouted when he pulled away. Amy pressed her fingers hard against her throbbing clit—her pussy felt all too empty without him inside, a tunnel of muscles grasping at nothing. Just a moment later, something wet landed on her ass, soaking the back of her panties, and then her dress fell back down over her legs. Two strong arms wrapped around her tenderly, kissed the back of her neck, nuzzled against the soft spot under her ear.

For a long moment, she let him warm her, gave herself into the feeling of peace and safety. But neither peace nor safety were high on Amariel's list of priorities and with a well-placed push against his chest, she whirled around, stepped on the breeches that were still hanging between his ankles and before Amy knew what was happening, he was toppling backward into the soft forest ground.

"Ow!" Gohan protested when she straddled him and pulled a dagger from her belt. She had it at his neck all too easily. "Hey!"

"It seems the human curses anachronistically, too." Amy

grinned down at him. Her long dark fair fell like a veil around her face. Playfully, she pressed the dagger against his Adam's apple and smirked.

"Come find me if you ever want to work for the other side, human," she smiled, then cocked her brows and bent low to brush a little kiss over his lips. "You haven't lived until you find out how we elves feast...."

Her knees were still weak when she raised herself up again, but Amy felt light as air as she hurried away into the forest. There was come on her ass and she had some allies to find. This weekend everything would go just the way she had always wanted it to go. It was her weekend, her forest, her game.

IN THREES

Elizabeth Coldwell

The first time I saw him I was on all fours on the bed, naked and gagged with my own panties. Mitchell had ordered me to wait in that position while he paid a quick visit to the bathroom, and I was doing as I was told. Just my luck that at that moment room service finally deigned to deliver the bottle of champagne Mitchell asked them to send up when we'd first booked in, nearly an hour before.

Hearing the rap on the door and the waiter announcing his presence outside, I called as best I could through my gag, trying to attract Mitchell's attention. He'd insisted I wait in silence till he returned, and I knew my poor backside would pay the price for this flagrant act of disobedience, but this was important. Unfortunately, the waiter must have taken my muffled noises as an invitation to come in, because the lock snicked open and he walked into the room, carrying an ornate silver ice bucket.

He said nothing as he looked at me, though I felt like his eyes were eating up the sight before him: my breasts, hanging down full and heavy; my asscheeks, already bearing the red marks of the spanking Mitchell had dished out as soon as he'd stripped me bare; my mouth, plugged with a wad of black silk. Did he know that was my own underwear, wet and fragrant from the juices that been flowing since Mitchell rang me at the gallery that afternoon and told me to meet him at the Charmont? A hot flush suffused my body, burning deepest on my cheeks and echoing the pulsing heat between my legs.

It didn't help that the man could have stepped straight out of the file in my brain marked HOT, DIRTY FANTASY GUYS. He'd most likely shaved before he came on shift, but now the beginnings of a heavy stubble prickled on his chin. His black hair was a little too long, curling against his shirt collar, and his olive-toned skin and dark eyes spoke of a Mediterranean heritage. He made me think of all the scenarios that turned me on the most: the ones where Mitchell held me down firmly and encouraged some other man to touch and stroke me in all the ways I liked the best, taking me to the brink of orgasm and back so many times all I could do was beg and sob and promise to do whatever the two of them wanted, as long as they let me come.

"I'll just put this down here, shall I?" he said, gesturing with his head in the direction of the antique dresser. His accent was more rainy Manchester than romantic Sorrento, but it didn't take the level of my filthy fantasizing down even a notch.

I just nodded, barely noticing that Mitchell had returned to the room and was already fumbling in his wallet for a no doubt hefty tip. Not that he needed to buy this man's silence. The expression on the waiter's face told me that not only did he like what he saw very much indeed, but also that this wasn't the first time he'd interrupted some explicit scene or other. After all, the Charmont prided itself on its discretion as a venue, and you didn't hang on to that kind of reputation for long if you employed staff who didn't know when to keep their mouths shut.

He left the room with slow, backward steps, taking one last good look at my naked curves and the submissive posture in which they were displayed. Even before the door shut behind him, Mitchell was unbuckling his belt and pulling it free of his trouser loops.

"What's our rule on silence, Lucy?" he asked, not even waiting for an answer as he strode toward me. "Six with the belt will help to enforce it, I think…."

Such a harsh punishment, but I deserved it. And I wondered, in the instant before the first blow fell, whether he realized all my thoughts were of the handsome waiter lashing my backside, while Mitchell looked on and told him to make sure I really felt every single one.

The second time I saw him, I was in a packed and sweaty rush-hour Tube carriage, and Mitchell had his hand down my leggings. We'd maneuvered ourselves through the crush of commuters into the best position for some fun: hard up against the glass partition by the door, where Mitchell could play with me unobserved. The game was simple: he would do his best to make me come with his skillful fingers, and I would try to show not a flicker of emotion as he teased and probed. Sometimes he made it a little easier for me by stroking me through my jeans, the friction of his touch dulled by a thick layer of denim. I could fight against the slow buildup of sensation, eyes closed tight so I couldn't see the smirk on his face as he worked to wring an orgasm from me.

Today, though, I had on the kind of clothing he could slip his hand into without fuss, working his fingers against the tight knot of my clit as the train rattled and jolted and tinny music leaked from the headphones of the man whose broad, T-shirted back I could see over Mitchell's shoulder.

When the waiter got on at South Kensington, I had to look twice to make sure it was really him. He'd never been far from my thoughts since that night at the Charmont, his stubbled features permeating those idle moments in the gallery when I closed my eyes and daydreamed of Mitchell punishing me in front of a willing voyeur. It shouldn't have surprised me to see him getting on at what was the closest Tube station to the hotel, but still I hadn't really expected our paths to cross again so soon.

He hadn't noticed me, or so I thought at first, as Mitchell's fingers continued to dance over my clit. The train came to a halt, and through force of habit I looked round in exasperation at the delay, even as the driver mumbled over the intercom that we were being held at a red signal and should be moving shortly. Our eyes locked; the connection was made. No doubt if we'd been close enough to speak, he'd have made some cheesy quip about not recognizing me with my clothes on. His gaze flashed over my body, lingering at crotch level, and I knew in that instant he'd realized what we were doing. He already knew Mitchell and me for the brazen game players we were: what more could he have expected from us than that I would let my lover frig me on a crowded train?

Burning under the intensity of his stare, driven to the brink by Mitchell's fingers, I didn't even try to hold back. As the train jolted into movement once more, I surrendered to the orgasm that rushed through my body. Fierce. Unstoppable. Observed by a stranger.

The third time I saw him, I was in the lobby of the Charmont, and I'd been waiting almost an hour and a half for him to appear. We'd been forced to close the gallery for the afternoon, due to the need to make emergency repairs to a fractured gas main in the street outside. Instead of heading home, some impulse sent me in the direction of the hotel where Mitchell and I enjoyed so many of our kinky trysts. Located halfway between his apartment and the gallery, it was an ideal meeting place for us, but this time it wasn't Mitchell I intended to meet there.

I could, I thought as I ordered a pot of tea from the hotel bar, be completely wasting my time. After all, I didn't even know whether the man would be working here today. But it was pleasant to sit in the beautifully restored Art Deco lobby, with its black-and-white-checkered marble floor and softly glowing brass light fixtures, and sip strong, milky Darjeeling while I distracted myself with pleasant daydreams of the last time Mitchell and I had booked in.

Lost in a reverie in which the waiter didn't just set down the ice bucket and leave, but came over to the bed to caress my sore, punished ass and run a finger down the crack between my cheeks to discover the wetness pooling in my pussy, at first I didn't notice him as he walked past.

His voice, low and insinuating, almost made me slop tea into my saucer as I realized he was addressing me. "We really are going to have to stop meeting like this. People will talk." He grinned, his hot gaze raking over me. "Waiting for your husband—boyfriend, whoever?"

I shook my head. "No, actually, I was waiting for you."

It obviously wasn't the answer he'd been expecting, but he only lost his composure for a moment. "Is there something I can help you with?"

"Yes. What time do you come off shift?"

He glanced at his watch. "In about fifteen minutes' time."

"Good. That gives you fifteen minutes to cancel whatever plans you had for tonight." If he thought I was joking, the look

I fixed him with seemed to convince him otherwise. I went on. "Fifteen minutes to wonder just what I'm going to let you do to me. Whether I'm wet enough for you to slip two fingers inside me, or three. Whether I take it up the ass. And whether I'll allow you to spunk in my face, or just over my tits."

"Fuck," he muttered under his breath. "I had you pegged as a dirty bitch, but…"

"You don't have to take me up on my offer, and you have to understand that if you do, you'll end up fucking me on my fiancé's bed, and he'll be there to do more than just watch. But if you do turn me down, you'll never be offered a second chance. What do you say?"

"Does he know about this? Is this something you do on a regular basis?" Despite all the questions, and the deliberate ambiguity I'd created about Mitchell's role in proceedings, he didn't sound like he was dismissing the idea out of hand.

"No, and no. But I'll have time to let him know while I wait for you to come off shift, and believe me, he won't have a problem with it." I looked round the lobby as if someone might be listening to what we were discussing, but the desk clerk was deep in conversation with a middle-aged female guest, pointing out some place of interest on a map. Though maybe this would be even better with an audience, I thought as I spread my legs just wide enough to give him a clear view up my dress. A view that revealed I wasn't wearing any underwear. I'd removed it and stuffed it in my handbag before leaving the gallery, needing to feel the breeze on my overheating pussy. I hadn't planned to use the sight as some kind of leverage to seal the deal—in truth, I didn't need to—but it sucked him in a little deeper, made it that bit harder for him to walk away.

He licked his lips, appearing to make some kind of internal decision. "Yeah, okay, I'm up for it. And I'm Lee, by the way."

The grin was back, stretching his lips a fraction wider than before. "Because you need to know what name to scream when I'm slapping your slutty little pussy."

The moment he'd gone, I reached for my phone, punching in Mitchell's number with trembling fingers. Any plans he'd had for a quiet evening in were ripped up the moment I told him we'd have a friend joining us. A friend who wasn't in the least fazed by my filthiest suggestions.

Even as the clock ticked toward six, I still expected Lee to back out. Given time to consider my proposition, let his head do the thinking instead of his dick, would he really think it a good idea to let a stranger take him home? So it surprised me to see him strolling in my direction across the lobby, elderly leather jacket over his uniform shirt and that slow, dirty grin spreading across his face.

"Okay, I'm all yours." He waited for me to stand. As we made our way toward the front door, my heels clicking on the marble, a waitress was already scurrying over to clear away the tea things.

We walked in silence, not because either of us was uncomfortable with the situation, but simply because we both seemed to recognize that swapping chitchat and personal information would break this weird, erotic spell that bound us. Lee had to be thinking about my knickerless state; I certainly was, all too aware that if he chose to back me up against a wall and thrust his hand beneath the skirt of my dress all he'd feel would be hot, slick woman flesh. I could almost smell my own arousal above the heavy scent of exhaust smoke and sun-warmed asphalt, and wondered whether he could, too.

Mitchell had promised to leave the front door on the latch, and true to his word, it opened at my touch. If Lee had any thoughts about the size of my fiancé's home, or its position in a sweeping Georgian terrace on a quietly expensive street, he kept them to himself. A girl who let her lover play with her cunt on public transport had already propositioned him; why should he be surprised when that lover turned out to own a house whose worth was valued in the millions?

I led Lee up the stairs and along the landing, pausing as we reached the bathroom. "You can take a shower first, if you'd like?" I suggested, my thoughts already turning to peering through a crack in the door, watching as he got naked and soaped himself down.

He shook his head. "Afterward, maybe...once I've worked up a sweat."

"Then start working on it." I all but pushed him into the bedroom, where Mitchell waited for us, propped up against the pillows and wearing only a towel around his waist. His cock made a solid, all-too-visible ridge in the fluffy white terry cloth. He lounged like some decadent Roman emperor waiting to discover what orgiastic delights had been laid on for his personal entertainment.

Lee took a couple of paces closer to the bed and the two men regarded one another, expressions inscrutable as they sized each other up. Butterflies whirled crazily in my stomach, as the reality of what I'd engineered struck home. Beginning to consider all the ways this situation could go wrong, I was stopped in my agitated mental tracks by Mitchell's voice.

"Strip her."

For the briefest of moments, I thought it might not happen. Then Lee's hand was around my waist, pulling me to him so he could tug down the zip of my dress. Keeping just on the right side of roughness, he yanked each strap off my shoulder. The garment puddled at my feet in a soft heap of Pucci-printed viscose, leaving me in nothing but nude lace bra and high heels.

"And where are your panties?" Mitchell's tone was that of the weary headmaster confronting a recalcitrant pupil, the tone that always let me know some kind of punishment was on the cards.

"In my handbag—Sir." I fought the urge to cover my crotch with my hands, knowing both men would be enjoying the sight of my pink mound, covered only by a thin strip of hair.

"And what kind of slut walks the streets without her panties on?" he continued.

"This kind, Sir." The kind that does it because you love it, I wanted to add. The kind who'll make some wild suggestion to a guy she's only seen twice about joining her and her lover for a threesome. The kind who hasn't been fully bared yet and is desperate to be.

As if sensing my unspoken need, Lee flicked open the front catch of my bra and let my breasts fall free of the cups. Almost before I knew it, he'd caught hold of my wrists and used the bra to tie them together behind my back. Though not in my plans, or Mitchell's as far as I knew, the impromptu bondage only served to make me wetter, more anxious for fulfillment.

Lee pushed me onto the bed. I landed facedown, my nose only inches away from Mitchell's terry-covered crotch. With a grin, he pulled the folds of toweling away, and I gazed on the fat bulk of his erect cock, the foreskin peeled away to reveal the tender core within. My mouth watered in response to the sight and smell of him.

"Suck me," he ordered, "and do a good job, or it'll be the worse for your ass."

Crawling into position wasn't easy, my movements hampered as they were by my bound wrists. But I got myself settled over Mitchell's dick, and ran my tongue over the head, just the quickest of flicks, to lap up the juice that welled from its tip.

"Not good enough, slut." Mitchell slapped my ass, with a crisp, upward stroke that stung only a little. In my eyeline, I saw movement; heard the rustling of clothing being removed. I'd wanted to watch Lee undress, but the two men had contrived to deny me that treat. Who'd set this whole thing up? I wondered, as I took more of Mitchell's length in my mouth. Who was in charge here?

Not me, that became all too clear, as I felt Lee's hands on my asscheeks, pulling them wide apart. Helpless to prevent myself being spread for his gaze, I could only imagine how I looked to him. He'd be able to see everything, even the dark, wrinkled star of my asshole. This was what I'd wanted, to be open and available for both men to use. And now I had Mitchell's cock in my mouth, leaking its salty juices as I sucked him, and Lee's hand probing between my legs, tracing the length of my crease.

"So how wet are you?" I heard him murmur, echoing the words I'd used at the Charmont. "Enough for two fingers, or three?"

My only answer was a moan around Mitchell's bulging cockhead as Lee began to open me up. I kept on trying to give Mitchell the best blow job I could, but the feeling of first one, then a second finger sliding into me proved a serious distraction. Every time I faltered in my task, Mitchell's response was to swat my ass hard. Combined with the feeling of Lee working a third digit into my stretched, slippery hole, it was making it impossible for me to retain any shred of control.

"And the answer is three," Lee growled in my ear. "Now, why doesn't that surprise me?"

The fingers were withdrawn, as if he'd proved his point. Deprived of that almost painful, desperately necessary fullness, I grumbled my disappointment around my mouthful of Mitchell. In response, Lee's long index finger pressed at the entrance to my ass. With an indecent lack of resistance, the tight ring opened up to let him in.

"Oh, yes, that's it," Lee said, almost as if he couldn't believe I'd offered up my most intimate places to him so easily. What—who—had he given up to be here with us now? A takeaway pizza in front of the TV? A night out with the lads? A date with some girl who had no idea what she'd been turned down in favor of? I didn't know; cared even less. Here I was, skewered on Mitchell's shaft at one end, Lee's finger at the other, obediently sucking cock like the good little submissive I was.

"Wait till you have your cock up there," Mitchell said, conducting a conversation with Lee over my head, discussing me as if I wasn't even in the room. I marveled at how even he kept his voice, given that my tongue was feathering over the head of his dick. "You won't believe how tight she is."

"I can't fucking wait, mate...."

They were discussing the niceties of where the condoms and lube were kept, but I'd tuned them out, focused only on the task of bringing Mitchell to his peak with my mouth. Without my hands free to caress his balls and wank his shaft with the short, fast strokes that always propelled him over the edge, I had to work twice as hard with my lips and tongue. He had to appreciate the effort I was putting in, but his only reaction was those sharp spanks to my ass, designed to spur me on to suck harder. And when his hips began to jerk and I knew he had to be close, he just gripped my hair in his fist and pulled my head off his cock.

"Not yet," he said. "I don't want to come till your ass is plugged full of his cock."

Guiding me by my hair, he encouraged me to look over my shoulder. I got my first sight of Lee's naked body. Lean and honey-tanned, with just enough muscle where it counted, and a long cock, already sheathed in taut black latex, rising from a nest of crisp, dark curls. Quite a lot to take in such a small hole, but I was ready for the challenge.

Mitchell unfastened my wrists from their makeshift bondage, knowing I'd need free use of my limbs for what was about to come, then held me steady as Lee clambered back on the bed, homing in on my upraised rump. I'd never been so conscious of my body: the heavy, downward drag of my breasts; the pulse beating in my clit; my nerves taut and expectant as I felt Lee's cockhead butt at the entrance to my ass. Bigger than any toy I'd ever been plugged with, thicker than Mitchell's so-familiar shaft, his dick pressed home slowly, relentlessly. I couldn't focus on anything but the sensation of being stretched almost to the point of pain, even though my lover's cock still bobbed in front of my pleasure-glazed eyes. Only when Lee stopped moving did I bend and take Mitchell into my mouth once more.

And for a moment I stayed like that, frozen so any onlooker could admire the submissive tableau I presented, filled at both ends. I'd been dreaming of this moment since Lee had agreed to my outrageous proposal, and now that it had happened I almost didn't know how to react.

Mitchell's cock twitched between my lips, reminding me how close he'd been before he'd called a halt to my oral ministrations. Lee's calloused hands grasped my buttocks, his thumb stroking the soft flesh absentmindedly. That faint motion roused me from the erotic torpor that gripped me, and I began to suck Mitchell again as Lee ground his hips against my ass.

At first, our movements were clumsy, out of sync, like a machine whose gears didn't quite mesh. Lee's thrusts pushed me hard onto Mitchell's length, and my teeth grazed his tender skin with a force that made him wince. I did my best to mumble an apology around his length. This wasn't going to work, not in the smooth, well-oiled way it always had in my fantasies, and I was on the verge of relinquishing my hold on Mitchell's dick and admitting defeat. But somehow, we managed to fall into the right rhythm, and my fears melted like ice in the summer sun. Two into one would go, it seemed.

Hot, salty cock in my mouth. Hard, thrusting cock in my ass. My own fingers free to reach between my thighs and rub at my clit with frantic motions. Lee's throaty grunts, Mitchell's moaning assertion that he was about to come. Too much sensation, too much pleasure.

Mitchell bucked beneath me, forcing even more of himself into my mouth. Lee never stopped thrusting, not for a moment, and I found myself drooling helplessly around the thickness of Mitchell's shaft, eyes tearing up, as he pumped his seed down my throat.

"She's all yours now," he muttered, slumping back against the pillows. Lee didn't reply, just kept plowing into me with long, relentless strokes. My eyes met Mitchell's, and what I saw there made me glow with love for him. Satisfaction, pride and admiration at the sight I presented to him, asshole stretched wide around another man's cock. I'd given myself to a stranger, but he was the one reaping the rewards.

"Nearly there now, nearly there," Lee chanted like a mantra, the words gradually dissolving into incoherence as the need to come engulfed him. Hard as I tried to time my orgasm to his, excitement propelled me on and I came first, losing the battle to keep staring into Mitchell's eyes as I did. My muscles clenched tight around Lee's dick and that did it for him; cursing and groaning, he came deep in my ass, the condom catching every drop.

Mitchell caught me as I fell forward, holding me tight and whispering his gratitude into my ear. "If this is how you're going to surprise me from now on, bring it on."

Lee was lying back on the bed, staring up at the ceiling as if he couldn't quite believe what he'd done.

"There's wine chilling on the dresser," Mitchell told him. "Help yourself. And there's cheese and crackers, too. I thought we might all need to keep our strength up."

I smiled to myself. Trust him to think of the practicalities, like drinks and snacks, while I'd been busy concentrating on kinkier matters. But that was why we made such a great team.

In our own way, we'd both been working to this moment since Lee had opened that hotel-room door. The first time, we'd intrigued him. The second, we'd convinced him. The third, we'd had him. Things came in threes, after all. And as Mitchell's fingers stroked over my clit, reawaking sensations that had barely had time to die away, I was pretty sure that before the evening had finished, I would be one of them.

THE CAKE

Ingrid Luna

He'll be here soon. The kitchen is growing warm, the mingling vanilla and sugar fill it up with a comforting smell. He loves the smell of vanilla, he has told me. I don't know why. Probably reminds him of his mother or something, I'm sure, as per usual. I crack the oven door carefully and peek inside. The cake is rising gorgeously, a soft golden pillow of moist sweetness. I have a momentary worry that it won't be perfect, but I calm myself quickly. It will be delicious. I'm a damn good baker. Slowly, I insert a toothpick into the heart of it. It comes out cleanly with just a few crumbs clinging. I lick them off.

"Done!" I exclaim happily, and can't resist a little victory dance there in the kitchen. The cake goes onto the smooth wooden cutting board to cool, and I go into the bedroom to change.

Off comes the battered Slayer shirt I live in when I'm not expecting company. I kick my jeans into a pile in the corner and strip off my ratty black underwear. I start the shower and rifle through my closet while the water heats up. The housedress perhaps? No, I wore that last time he visited. The halter dress with the large circle skirt isn't quite right. I remember he said something about an aversion to seersucker. Finally, I find the lavender silk dress I snapped up at my favorite vintage shop last month. I had completely forgotten about it, and it hung dejected on its velvet hanger.

"Let's see what he thinks of you," I coo, twirling it around in front of me.

Fifteen minutes later I stand in front of my full-length mirror, admiring my transformation. My usually messy mane tamed into red fox curls coiled gently above the smooth white skin of my forehead, the lavender dress clinging to every curve of my admittedly ample bust before nipping in dramatically at the waist and then exploding in a full skirt just below my knees. I have a pretty marvelous hourglass shape naturally, but today it seems almost cruel, really, thanks to the corset I have struggled into. I am all dangerous racetrack curves. I balance the effect of all of this with a pale lip and nude stockings. He likes me to be a tad subtle. A subdued, accidental sexiness.

I pout into the mirror, practicing wholesome and coy. It's a challenge for me, to be honest.

Back in the kitchen, the cake is ready to be iced. Softened butter works its magic with sugar and a little cream. I'm going to make a butterscotch icing. It's my favorite. The rest of the ingredients go into the mixing bowl where the beaters work away at them—that magical kitchen alchemy I love. Soon the frosting is standing up in fluffy peaks and I spoon it out onto my cake in great creamy globs, smoothing it expertly with a broad knife. It's immaculate, my cake. Homey and simple but exquisitely executed. Of course. That's one of the reasons he keeps coming back.

By the time he arrives, I am perfumed and the kitchen is spotlessly clean. A gin gimlet perspires gently in my hand, soft jazz is twinkling softly through the house and the cake is resting on white china on the sturdy kitchen table.

"Darling!" I exclaim, looping my arms around his neck and kissing him gently on the cheek. "You're back! I'm so happy to see you!"

"Hello, lovely," he says, and takes my shoulders in his hands, turning me around gently. "You look perfect. How beautiful. Is this a new dress?"

I manage a tiny shy smile, averting my eyes. "Yes. Do you like it? It isn't...too tight?" I run my hands over my narrow rib cage, his eyes following their movement. For a moment, there is nothing but pure lust in his eyes. He coughs slightly and looks a little embarrassed.

"It smells wonderful in here!"

"Oh yes! I nearly forgot! I made you a cake! Here, my dear, let me take your jacket."

As I pull it off of his large shoulders, I can't help but admire him. I've never asked his exact age, but I imagine him to be in his early fifties. He is nicely muscled, though, and everything about him implies that this is a man who takes care of himself and is used to getting his way. His shoes are always the finest leather, his suits obviously bespoke. I have never seen a stray hair, a wrinkle.

He rolls up his sleeves, exposing a watch that probably cost twice what my car did, and a hairy, muscular forearm.

"Shall we then?"

He takes my arm and leads me into the kitchen.

"Oh, you've truly outdone yourself, Charlotte. This is a thing of beauty for sure," he says, eyeing the cake like a goldsmith, as he sits at the simple wooden chair I have pulled out for him. I lean over his shoulder so that he can get a noseful of my perfume, and breathe into his ear, "I made it especially for you. I slaved away all afternoon and do you know what I was thinking about, the whole time?"

"I can guess."

"Well, go on then," I say, smiling sweetly.

"Actually, on second thought. Maybe you should show me. Are you ready, my turtle dove?"

"If you like."

He offers me his hand and I take it delicately. One dainty step up after another and then I am perched on the table in front of him. I can feel him admiring the aristocratic turn of my ankle, the lovely hue of my tasteful heel.

"Remove your tie," I instruct him.

I make a noose at each end, slide the rich fabric over one wrist and then the other, tying the ends securely to the chair arms. He can't move his hands an inch. I have him exactly where I want him.

The cake sits smugly between my shoes as I ruck my skirt up to my waist and unsnap the crotch of my apricot silk panties. I tuck them up into my garter, send him a shy little wink and slowly squat down until the lips of my shaved pussy are nearly touching the flawless frosting. I'm not turned on yet. There is just the faintest tingle in my belly, but he is captivated. He moves closer toward me, getting an eyeful as I ease ever closer to the buttercream.

Then, I simply sit.

The frosting engulfs my pussy and ass. I feel it gushing up under my skirt, coating my inner lips. The crack of my ass is speckled with frosting. My clit is coated with butterscotch and chunks of still-warm cake are trying to work their way inside me. I grind down on it, using my fingers to spread it over my mound, massaging frosting into the pale soft skin at the top of my thighs. I run a finger through the ruined cake and spread it across my labia, then bring the finger to my mouth.

"Mmmmmmm..." I breathe, tasting the perfect combination of frosting, moist cake and pussy. I hold out my finger to him. "Would you like to try it?" He can't speak. I watch as this powerful, elegant man becomes as weak as a kitten with desire. I want to giggle. I feel a rush of heat between my legs. He nods, opening his mouth just a little, leaning toward the morsel I offer.

"Uh-uh." Pop goes the finger into my mouth. "No cake for you. You've been a very bad boy."

He whimpers slightly, neck still craned toward me, his tongue slightly between his teeth. He looks ridiculous. He shakes his head slightly.

"No?" I raise a sculpted eyebrow at him. "No? You've been a good boy? I don't think so. You've been thinking all kinds of naughty, terrible things. Haven't you?"

He shakes his head, stronger this time.

This is starting to get fun. I continue, "You want me to believe you are a good boy, worthy of this delicious confection? You want me to let you have some?"

I grab a handful of cake from between my legs.

"You disgusting, weak little pervert. You terrible, naughty thing. You speck of a man."

His cock is growing hard, I can see the shape of it clearly outlined through the fine fabric of his slacks.

I hold the cake an inch from his trembling lips and then snatch it back.

"I don't think you really want it," I scold, and drop the chunk of cake onto the floor.

"Oh I do! I do want it! I need it! Please, please let me have some! I'll be good! Just a taste!" he whines. He's practically weeping.

I slide my legs over his shoulders, balancing myself on the edge of the table with one hand, and grab the back of his head.

"You make me want to puke," I snarl. My pussy is a foot away from him. He can hardly contain himself as he eyes my rosy snatch through the buttercream. "You are the most vile, pathetic creature. You aren't worthy of one bite of this cake I made. But you know what? I'm going to let you have a little taste because I am feeling very very generous today."

I pull his head roughly into me. He begins to eat. His tongue laps up the frosting, his lips smack at my cunt.

"Oh...that's better. That's what nice boys do. Do you like that? Does it taste good?"

He says something but it's impossible to understand. His mouth is full of cake and cream and me.

"You're doing a very good job down there. I'm going to let you have some more."

I smear another gob of cake onto my pussy and he continues to work at me. He eats ravenously, sucking at my clit and sliding his tongue inside me, trying to get every last crumb. His mouth seems to be everywhere. I'm going to come soon. I cling to his hair, pressing his face into my slit.

"That's a good boy. Eat your cake. Eat it. I want to be cleaner than clean when you're done. If I find even a trace of icing down there I'm going to punish you!"

He slurps at me, running his tongue down the crack of my ass and expertly nibbling and licking his way back to my clit.

My orgasm rips through me like an electric shock. Letting go of his head, I fall back on the table and gasp as it floods through me. He leans forward, straining against his bonds, still hungry for me.

I can't help it. I start to giggle. His regal face is messy with desire and frosting.

"Oh, look at you. Let me get a napkin." I climb down from the table and untie him. He rubs his sore wrists as I arrange my skirt.

My kitchen is a wreck. Cake is everywhere. I hand him the napkin, and he wipes his face.

He is composed again though there is a small, wet stain near his zipper. I wonder if he has a wife, and if she'll notice.

"Thank you, Charlotte," he says. "Same time next week?"

PUNISHING DESDEMONA

Catherine Paulssen

"No! No no no no no," Kenneth yelled, turned his eyes away from the stage and impatiently slapped a script he was holding rolled up in his fist against a chair in the row in front of him.

He jumped up and walked over to the pair of actors, the younger of whom was almost frozen, the woman on all fours before him carrying an unfazed but slightly tired expression on her face.

"Jerome," Kenneth addressed the guy. "You're madly in love with your woman. She's independent, she's hot, and she's so much more experienced than you. People keep telling you she's doing you wrong with one of your best friends, only exacerbating the voices in your head that have been plaguing you with jealousy and doubt ever since she said she was yours." He eyed him expectantly. "You're burning with anger and disgust— toward yourself, toward Desdemona, but most of all toward the love that binds you to her. You got that?"

Jerome looked uncomfortable but nodded.

"Now this is Othello's fantasy. Your chance to let the audience in on his wildest dreams of revenge," Kenneth went on. "Show them how much you want to make Desdemona yours. Show them how much you want to get back at her for doing you wrong. Let out all your pent-up frustration. I want to hear the smacks, even in the farthest seat in the back, got it?"

Jerome gulped. "It's just that—"

"I want to hear them!" Kenneth repeated. "I want to see her body flying forward, I want to feel the impact when your hand hits her butt."

He turned and walked back into the auditorium, leaving Jerome to cast a doubtful glance at the perfect round cheeks presenting themselves to him. His huge dark hands seemed so inappropriate on the tender skin, as misplaced as a blotch of mud staining a meadow of freshly fallen snow. He licked his dry lips as his eyes wandered over the perfect curves of Diana's back, the tight skin over her spine enticing his fingers to trace its small peaks. He regarded the soft hairs where back met bottom, admiring them as they shimmered in the harsh shine of the spotlights. What he would do...what he could do if—?

"Come on," Diana said, interrupting his thoughts. She gave him a gentle nod with her head. "You can do it." Her face was half-covered by wild curls, but he could still make out the impish smile that creased her features. "Just imagine I was a very naughty girl last night."

She turned and got into position again, wiggling her exquisite butt at him, and he could hear her giggling softly.

"Let me hear your fury," Kenneth's voice roared from the last row.

Jerome closed his eyes and drew a short breath. He loved her with all he had. She was doing him wrong. He was furious. He was hurt. He would tame her. He would mark her. He wouldn't let her forget who she belonged to.

Most of all, he would show her how precious she was to him.

He raised his hand and brought it down on Diana's cheek, but even as he did it, he could tell he was restraining himself from really hitting her hard. When his hand met her skin, it was no more than a slap, and even before Kenneth started to curse, he could hear Diana's disappointed groan.

He lowered his gaze and waited for Kenneth's outburst to end. "Couldn't we—maybe with sound effects…" Jerome made a feeble attempt to get out of tainting Diana's fair skin, but Kenneth wouldn't have it.

"Sound effects," he spat. "I want to show a whole new Othello. One who is in charge. One who doesn't let himself be pushed around. Of course in the end, he'll lose his battle with jealousy and betrayal, but until then, I want him to be raw. He's human, yes, but he's fighting his human frailty. Got me?"

Jerome nodded.

"That's why I want just you and the audience. No special effects, no gimmicks of any kind. Just your emotions, stripped and bare. You're doing a good job showing me his vulnerable side," the director continued, his voice a bit softer now. "But for this scene, I need to see the war hero, the redoubtable general in the Venetian army, the Othello who would never let his woman act up on him."

As he rode the bus home that night—the scene not rehearsed to either his own or Kenneth's satisfaction—Jerome kept going over the director's words in his head. "Independent, hot, much more experienced… You love her…"

He exhaled and watched his breath fog the cold bus window. This was nothing he needed to be told. More than fifteen years his senior, Diana was a stunning woman. She had a smoky voice with a fruity, smooth ring to it. Legs that went on and on, accentuated with slim-cut ankle pants and high heels. Huge eyes framed by a voluminous bunch of tight curls—eyes that looked at him with an expression he couldn't read. He detected a sort of collegial affection, curiosity and something else that made him wonder if he could ever be more to her than just an aspiring actor.

Never had a woman got his head spinning like Diana did. And when she crouched before him during the dream sequence wearing nothing but a thong and sheer lace-top stockings, her butt perked up so seductively, all kinds of bewildering thoughts ran through his head that made it hard for him to focus on anything else.

It confused him that she could still exude an air of being in complete control, of majesty almost, even as she assumed the most humble and submissive position.

As soon as she stopped acting the part of Desdemona, Diana would treat him with an attitude that—with every gesture, with every move—told him she thought he was cute and adorable... like a little boy. It upset and infuriated him. Yes, he was at the beginning of his career, fresh out of acting school, and this play was his first real chance at the big leagues. But he wasn't a child. He had had his share of experiences. Given the chance, he knew he could prove himself to her. He lost himself in reveries and almost missed the bus stop.

When he arrived at rehearsal the next day, he heard her gravelly voice even before he saw her. It had an unusual honeyed ring to it, and his stomach gave a little flip at the sultry sound, but this was immediately followed by a sucker punch to the gut as he heard a deep male voice respond.

Gaz.

One of the extras.

Broad shouldered, square chinned, oozing blue-collar charm.

How he hated him.

Envied him at the same time.

He turned the corner, and the first thing that caught his eye were Gaz's strong hands around Diana's waist, holding her tight, the tanned calloused skin a dramatic contrast against her plain white T-shirt. She had her arms wrapped around his neck and was whispering into his ear, causing him to laugh smugly and spin her around.

Did her eyes meet his as she was swung?

She traced the lines of Gaz's collarbone and temple with her slender finger. Was it that sight that rooted him to the spot, or did he simply not want to move? He didn't know, and he didn't care. Now he was sure she had noticed his lean figure in the corner, for when she pressed a peck on Gaz's ear, her eyes fixed on Jerome.

"I'll see you at lunch," she whispered with a final nuzzle at Gaz's earlobe before she turned and vanished.

Gaz passed Jerome as he walked away, a satisfied grin on his face.

If she had been trying to get him into his character's mood, she hadn't succeeded. Not that by lunch he hadn't cooked up several plots in which Gaz met an untimely end. And not that the humiliation of being a hopeful young actor paired with some of the biggest names in the business and not living up to the expectations placed upon him didn't nag at him. And definitely not that the furious desire to show Diana that he appreciated her so much more than anybody else didn't burn at his very core.

But even later that day, when it was time for the dream sequence and she awaited him on all fours, her nipples erect in the theater's chilly air and just visible beyond her armpits, her ass so inviting, he couldn't do it. The position into which she was hunched, her nakedness and her grace made him want to do so many things, made him wish she was alone with him, offering herself that willingly, allowing him to reward her for her submission to his loving hands—but he wouldn't slap her sweet butt with the force his character's anger required.

Such a woman—such an ass—deserved to be loved not beaten.

That's what it all came down to, in his mind.

Kenneth was at the end of his patience. "Jerome, what's your problem, man?" A moment later, he was on stage standing next to Jerome. He raised his own hand by way of demonstration, aimed—and slapped Diana's butt with a force that made Jerome gulp and sent a shiver through Diana's delicate body.

"You hear that?" Kenneth asked. He spanked her again, and Jerome winced as Kenneth's stubby fingers clashed with Diana's left cheek, leaving a red imprint. The smack reverberated from the stage walls and filled the hall. Kenneth planted another blow, this time on her right cheek, and then one more. Each whack hit her with such impact her arms almost gave out beneath her. Jerome expected her to whimper. He waited for her to demand that Kenneth stop, but she merely groaned softly.

"See how it's done?" Kenneth asked, as if he had just taught Jerome how to prepare good tenderloin. Jerome nodded, not looking at him. He couldn't turn his eyes away from Diana's maltreated behind.

She sighed, and Jerome watched the skin Kenneth had smacked turn from red to pink. He shuddered wondering how much it must have hurt her, and when Kenneth jumped from the stage, he shyly placed his hand on the tender flesh and stroked it. He could feel the heat the spanks had aroused, and inside of him, he felt a sudden urge to kiss the spots and soothe her pain. Diana raised her ass—it was only by a bit, but to him, it felt as if she were snuggling her sore flesh into the palm of his hand. Now she turned her face toward him and smiled. "Do it."

He cupped one cheek in his huge hands and squeezed it lightly. Would he?

Some noise in the auditorium made him turn. In the diffuse light, he could make out several figures. Apparently, everyone who hadn't anything better to do was keen to watch him fail.

Now the spotlight was directed on him, and he could feel beads of sweat forming at the nape of his neck. He bit his lip and landed a tentative smack on Diana's butt.

He wanted to vanish into a haze and never return.

His anger rising—had he heard someone laughing?—he let another strike follow and another and another. He was half beside himself with anger, but even in his frantic state, he could tell they didn't have half of Kenneth's firmness, nor his accuracy. They weren't, he knew, at all what the director was looking for.

Panting, he stopped and turned toward the auditorium.

Kenneth shook his head, and Jerome could feel the taut air fill the theater. One of the prop masters sneered.

"We'll take it from here tomorrow," said Kenneth, throwing Jerome an exasperated look before rising from his seat and leaving the theater.

The small crowd shuffled out, Diana stood up and wrapped a terry-cloth robe around her body, and the spotlight was turned off. But Jerome remained standing there on the empty stage.

He was the world's biggest fool, wasn't he? Fellow students from his acting class would kill for the chance he'd been given, and he knew he was perfect for the role. So was he really messing it up because he couldn't find a way to channel his confusion, doubts and self-loathing?

Minutes passed, and when he was sure he wouldn't run into any of them anymore on his way out, he left the hall, got himself a bottle of water from a vending machine, then trotted on through the windowless, neon-lit corridor.

"Are you scared, lover boy?"

He stopped short at the sound of a voice coming from the other side of a door. Next thing he knew, he was being dragged into the small room behind it—Diana's wardrobe.

His eyes grew accustomed to the dim light shed by an old-fashioned table lamp, and he looked around the sparsely furnished room. In its corner stood a huge mirror next to a plain wooden table that she used as a vanity stand. Framed posters from former productions stared down at him from the salmon-colored walls. Above a plushy white sofa, a rectangular window overlooked the theater's backyard; big drops of rain pressing themselves against its pane were the only sound to be heard.

Diana leaned against the opposite wall, dressed again in her skinny jeans and plain white shirt.

"Let's practice," she said simply, coming toward him and taking the water bottle and bag out of his hands. Placing these on the floor, she turned and leaned against the windowsill.

"Come on. Spank me." She offered him her butt.

He hesitated, but when she perked up her bottom a bit farther, he delivered a halfhearted blow on her jeans-clad cheeks.

"Harder, baby."

He rolled his eyes. "This feels stupid."

She straightened up and looked at him inquiringly. Her cocoa-colored irises hadn't lost any of their calm. "Fine," she said. "Then let's get down to it."

He watched her incredulously as she unzipped her pants and

stepped out of them. "Would you like me to keep the shoes on?" she asked lightly.

"Diana…"

A grin flashed over her face. "I can tell you're the type of man who likes a naked woman in heels."

His heart beat faster. What she had said, the way she had said it… It aroused him even more than the prospect of seeing her naked again.

Without an audience, this time.

She stripped off her shirt. Holding his gaze, she wrapped one of her long legs around him and pressed her almost-naked body against his. Her finger played with a strand of his hair, then moved across his cheek down to his chin and neck. Jerome could taste her breath on his mouth.

"Baby, I know you have it in you…" she whispered. She breathed a kiss on his lips, but before he could wake up from the spell she'd cast and deepen that kiss, she had turned around and was rubbing her bottom against his crotch. His cock reacted immediately, bobbing against his jeans. His first impulse was to free it from the pants' restraints, push her down on the sofa and show her what he had in him. But Diana took his hand and pressed it against her buttcheek. He grabbed it, but she took a step forward and eluded his grip. As she had done earlier, she wiggled her ass, her hands running through her hair, pulling the curls up and letting them fall back on her shoulders.

"Make it yours, Jerome," she whispered. The lights of a car leaving the yard flickered over her silhouette, painting it silvery-blue for a moment. She repeated his name, and he detected a soft longing in the way she uttered its syllables. Before he knew it, he could hear the crack of flesh meeting flesh and the warmth as blood rushed through his palm. The room fell back into semi-darkness.

Diana purred, and for a moment, he caught sight of her tightened nipples through her bra.

Had he really spanked her? He must have. He could feel the tingling shooting into his fingertips. But what overwhelmed him even more was the sudden realization that she...

He parted her legs with his hand and ran his fingers over the soft skin between her thighs. She shuddered a little and drew a hissing breath as he moved the tip of his thumb over her pussy.

Even through the mesh of her thong, he could tell how aroused she was.

"You like this," he blurted out.

She half turned, a sly grin on her face. "I might."

His breath caught in his throat. "You're enjoying this?"

She shrugged.

"You...and all the while I thought I was hurting you!"

"Hurting me?" She threw her curls back and laughed.

Her laughter infuriated him. He had tried to be considerate. He had tried not to make her skin burn. He had tried not to take the play too far. "Bend over," he said, suddenly firm.

"What?" she asked.

"Bend over," he repeated slowly. His cock jolted when she did, and swelled even more when she raised her buttcheeks higher. She propped her hands against the vanity table and waited for him to make the next move.

Lightly, he brushed her bottom with his fingers, then pulled off her thong, making sure she felt the tickling touch of his fingertips as he removed the lacy thing. Diana had stopped moving, the wriggling with which she had teased him now gone completely. She had noticed the change that had occurred within him, and Jerome was sure she was even holding her breath. As he drew circles over her skin, goose bumps emerged in their wake. They grew more pronounced in the whiff of cold air that brushed her butt as he let his hand come down on her cheek once again with all the force he could muster.

She moaned as his fingers left their mark on her skin. The next smack followed almost immediately.

Jerome pressed his hand against the spot he had just hit, making her feel the heat for as long as possible. He traced the line of her spine down to the crack of her butt, wondering what had happened in the last few minutes. All of a sudden, he couldn't wait to give her the next blow, and he found his mind figuring out ways to make sure she got the most out of it. He wanted her to secretly beg, or maybe even very openly beg. He needed her to be unable to stay patient much longer, and he wanted the next smack to come as a surprise when it finally hit her.

But if she was yearning to be spanked again, she didn't show it. The only sign was her ragged breath, which he could hear emerging from underneath her thick curls. She pulled herself together, surrendering complete control to him.

He spread her legs a bit farther apart so that he could better feel the dampness of her slim strip of bushy hair. His hand crawled up her inner thighs, then over the part where her butt met her thighs. Now was the moment. He knew it, and he could tell she was literally willing him to spank her.

His hand whizzed through the air and came down on her left cheek, the pain stinging his open palm the moment it struck her round, curvaceous sweetness. Her moaning grew more intense, and Jerome let a few spanks follow, the first ones hard and fast, the next more gentle, ending in an almost caressing slap. Even in the dim light, he could tell that her ass was burning. He could see the difference in color between her left and her right cheek. The pale, bare virginity of the right one tempted him, but he needed a short interlude, and he knew she did too.

"Did you like that?" he asked, just to say something, because her whole body gave away just how much he had turned her on.

She answered with an undefined grunt, then turned around and smiled at him. Her hand wandered to the bulk in his pants, and she started to massage him gently. "I knew you would like it too," she chuckled. She searched his eyes. "And now that you've tasted it, you want more, don't you?"

Instead of giving an answer, he pulled her hand away and pressed her against the table with gentle force. "I'm just giving you what you've longed for all along," he whispered and teased her right cheek, grazing it with his fingernails. "And what you deserve."

But that wasn't the full truth. He did want more. And he was looking forward to turning her into putty beneath his hands, to making her right cheek sting as much as her left one. "And you long for more too, don't you?" he asked.

She uttered an unwilling groan but got back into position. He was giddy with joy. How had he mastered a game that as recently as an hour ago, he never thought he'd play? What was it about her surrender that tempted him to savor it to the fullest? What was so intoxicating about knowing how much pleasure she derived from something he had thought was only painful?

She shivered as he took his hand away and for a moment, he kept it raised in the air so that he could enjoy her anticipation for as long as he could curb his own excitement. He placed his other hand on the small of her back, and under it he could feel impatience get the better of her as she squirmed underneath his grip—but only tentatively, never crossing the line to disobedience. He grew cocky now, and instead of giving her the release she craved, he let his fingers trail along her slit, pressing against her clit with tender force.

"Jerome," she gasped against the tabletop.

"Yes?"

"Do it already." She wriggled her cheeks.

"What?"

"Spank me," she begged. "Please."

He let his hand crash down on her butt, reddening her right cheek with one forceful slap of his open palm. The next blows followed quickly; he delivered whacks on her bare flesh until her cries of ecstasy were muffled by how hard she had to concentrate to absorb the intensity of his final smacks.

"Enough, baby?" he asked lovingly.

She nodded, unable to answer as her body hummed in the aftermath of the spanking she had received.

Jerome massaged his wrist. His cock pressed against his pants, but for a moment, while she brushed damp curls out of her face and regained her breath, he enjoyed just watching her red, swollen bottom. He brushed both cheeks lightly with the back of his hand, proudly taking in the heat. She certainly wouldn't be forgetting his rough treatment any time soon.

Next, he began to caress her back, soothing her, calming her down until the quivers that shook her body grew quiet.

When he felt that she was ready for more, he slowly unbuckled his belt, opened his jeans and sighed with relief. Teasingly, he rubbed the tip of his cock against her wet slit. Diana moaned longingly, and it was nearly impossible for him to keep himself from plunging into her right away and taking her hard.

Instead, he continued to circle her teasingly while his other hand petted the warm, sore skin of her butt.

She pushed her bottom back, prompting him to enter her already, but instead of complying, he bent over and parted her curls.

"Diana?" he whispered into her ear.

"Hm?" she said, in more of a breathless utterance than a reply.

Jerome cupped her butt more firmly. "Don't expect me to go easy on you at rehearsal tomorrow."

MONSOON SEASON

Valerie Alexander

We met on a hot, windy, dust storm of a night. It was early summer, and my best friend was holding her engagement party at a five-star resort. But a gritty cloud of dust blew into Phoenix that evening and when I arrived, the palm tree fronds were tossing above the hotel and leaves were skittering across the parking lot. My headlights illuminated a boy lounging at the parking valet stand: dark hair pushed back from high cheekbones, a defiant mouth. We looked at each other through my windshield, and then I pulled into a non-valet space.

I wanted to pretend I hadn't seen him yet. I wanted there to be an obstacle between us, so I could process what felt like a continent breaking apart inside me. Five months earlier my husband had moved out and I said to my best friend then, "Bring on the sex parade. I don't even want to know their names." I was unwilling to feel intensely about anyone or anything. But there he was, a spectacle of fuck-puppy lusciousness carving his face into my heart.

The smell of ozone was sharp as I got out of the car. It was monsoon season in Arizona, when thunderstorms were supposed to be breaking and cleansing the nights, but we were suffering a long drought and this summer had been dry and tense like a rubber band about to snap. The half-storm building tonight was just wind, heat and dust that gave an amber tint to the resort golf course lights. My hair had been straightened and highlighted for this party, and I'd been worried for the last hour about the dust storm ruining it, but now all I could think about was staying steady on my spike heels as I walked toward him.

He was still leaning coolly against the valet stand, with that impassive poker face boys use in their early twenties to hide their twisted, yearning hungers. I felt inexplicably tongue-tied—confident me, who liked to dominate men in bed until they crawled and begged for my favor, was somehow dismantled by a pretty kid. His jaw was rigid as he put down his cigarette.

First words should be portentous but ours were *I'm here for the Inzer-Trujillo engagement party* and *It's in the Saguaro Ballroom, I can show you. By the way, I'm Colton.* I took it as a sign that whatever happened between us would be casual and not especially verbal.

He came over the next night like a proper date. Clean T-shirt on and a bottle of wine in his hands, which I accepted before saying, "I don't want to open it right now, though."

Colton looked disappointed. I couldn't explain that I needed him sober, needed to know how willing and ready he really was for all the dark magic spells I wanted to unleash on him. Bossing him around, pulling him over my knee and spanking him, slapping his beautiful mouth just before he came. I had no logical reason for thinking he was sexually submissive, or that he'd done anything like that before, but then again, our animal hearts know what they know.

"Where would you like to go to dinner?" He was formal and polite.

I leaned back on my enormous black couch. "We can go out later. If we're hungry."

He looked at me with suspicion and uncertainty. I remembered that he was over a decade younger than me and probably nervous. So I patted the sofa and ordered him to sit with enough authority that he instantly obeyed.

His lean, rangy body felt like my property already. Like it was a time-lapse error that I hadn't officially fucked him yet. I looked over his dark hair and sun-bronzed cheekbones, his hard tattooed forearms. My hormones careened like drunken fireflies.

"I'm going to have my way with you now, and you're going to obey and do everything I say," I told him. "Understand? If you have any objections, say them now."

His body was so stiff. His voice the whisper of an echo as he said, "No objections."

I unwrapped him like a present, pants off first, followed by his navy boxer-briefs. His thigh muscles were almost as rigid as his cock. I could guess at the kind of sex he was used to having, the masterful young seducer, suave in his technique and just a little more detached than the girls wanted him to be. Which was why his poker face was so tight with control now as I pulled the front of his T-shirt up and behind his head and then down his back to bind his arms at his sides.

Now he was porn: the naked and half-bound boy with a hard, scarlet cock. I wanted to take his picture, but we weren't there yet. Instead I climbed onto his lap and pulled up my dress.

"Consider this an audition," was an arrogant thing to say as I pushed my pussy into his face. But his mouth ransacked me with feverish thirst, confirming that just maybe he did like to be bossed around by dominant women. I spread my knees open as his tongue pushed inside me with such energetic desperation that I suspected it would ache later. His arms struggled against the shirt until I rapped his ear in admonition. "None of that," I said. "Mouth only."

His hands clenched helplessly at his sides. I pushed his head back against the sofa and pulled my hood back from my clit. I leaned back just enough to make him work for it, a test of the agility and control of his tongue, and then gripped his hair and rode his face, a dreamy euphoria melting through my cunt. Brief, searing waves broke through me, blotting out the world for a few seconds.

I fell back on the cushions and caught my breath. His eyes searched my face for a sign of approval. His cock was so hard it looked painful.

I got up and straightened my dress. "I changed my mind. Let's get dinner now."

Betrayal and incredulity flashed through his eyes. Clearly no one had dared to ignore his hard-on before. But he got up and dressed slowly, as if hoping for a reprieve. I pretended to sort through my faux crocodile bag, an unexpected rejuvenation making me light-headed. It was rare for me to feel truly intoxicated by anyone, let alone find a beautiful submissive boy who was meeting every item on my domme's wish list. So I was more pleased at our chemistry than I wanted to let on.

It felt romantic to eat tapas by candlelight in a dark wooden room. Like any two people on a first date, we exchanged details. He had just moved to Arizona, had traveled around a bit. He described his new motorcycle to me for a painfully long time, but on the whole he was more intelligent and composed than I expected. If he was rattled by the twelve years between us or getting topped, he didn't show it.

When I came back from the restroom, he was waiting for me with a clever smile. "Look." He showed me the huge wooden spoon he'd stolen from a bowl of sangria.

It was an eternity of red lights before we got back to my house. We were barely in my front door when I pushed him against the wall and pulled his jeans down to his knees, liberating his hard dick. I gave him three smacks with the spoon right there, his ass pale in the dark and cool enough to contrast with the flaming print of the spoon. Then it was down to the sofa, him squirming over my knee and groaning like a boy should as I wielded the spoon with one hand and pulled his cock in my other. He was jerking wildly as he struggled not to come. I no longer needed to ask if he had done this with anyone before. Together we were perfect.

Dark skies gathered over Arizona, the occasional rumbling a tease and a lie. Because I telecommuted and didn't have to suffer rush-hour traffic, thunderstorms had always been a luxury for me. Watching the oleander shake and glow a preternatural green as sheets of rain obscured the glass felt serene. But the rain wasn't coming this summer and I paced the house every afternoon, feeling restless. Only when Colton arrived did my nerves settle. Because this was his first summer in Phoenix and the heat tired him out, I kept the house well chilled. I liked giving him baths in cool water, lathering him up and sculpting his dark hair into devil horns.

"Aren't you...?" He cleared his throat. "Normally, isn't it the, uh, sub who grooms the domme?"

It was cute to hear BDSM lingo come out of his mouth. Even cuter to think of him doing research online to find some framework for what he'd already called an addiction. "Not always. And I like taking care of you. Like you're my pet."

At least I wanted to think of him as my pet. But really Colton was becoming both a muse and something more. I kept dreaming up scenes involving blindfolds, spreader bars, his lean but muscular torso wrapped in chains. I wanted to tie him to my desk and play with him all day long as I worked, wanted to fuck him while he was wearing my underwear.

"Don't move."

That night I cuffed Colton's wrists behind his back and went to the kitchen to pour myself a drink. I sipped it when I returned, admiring him in his black thigh-high stockings and dog collar, his mouth taped shut. His cock was hard but he didn't even twitch.

I put my drink down and sucked his dick, tight and deep, until he was moaning through the tape. Then I let him drop and retrieved his phone from his pants, snapping a picture.

"Aw, look at you in black stockings, all handcuffed and gagged with your dick hard," I said. "Maybe I should send this to everyone in your phone."

His face turned the same burning crimson as his cock. I took the phone into my bedroom, letting him hang in the thrilling horror of potential humiliation, though he knew I would never actually send it. When I returned, he rolled onto his back and thrust his cock skyward. He was straining against his cuffs, leaking silvery webs of precome. He looked like he'd been kidnapped, like he was facing execution.

Suspicion confirmed: exposure was one of his most potent turn-ons. I straddled him, alternately playing with and slapping his hard cock, then rubbed his blood-darkened crown on my clit to the sound of his heartfelt, pleading groans through the tape. I traced his head around my slit, torturing myself and him before sitting on him and feeling his cock push up inside me like a velvet bar. He was squirming and groaning on the carpet now, all discipline lost as I succumbed to the dizzy euphoria of a pussy full of dick. I loved the helplessness and the heat of him bound like this, nothing more than a slave or a pet as I rode him with one hand over his mouth, his dark eyes burning and begging me to let him come.

"Remember," I said as we took another bath together the next night, "This isn't going to go on forever."

His wet shoulders tensed. "What does that mean?"

"It means everything changes." I kissed his ear, which was the shape and color of a small conch shell. "It means this kind of—voltage—can't go on indefinitely."

Colton didn't understand the compliment I'd just paid him. His face shifted into a moody pout, which I found heart melting though he didn't intend it to be such, and he was short with me the rest of the night. But he still slept over and I stayed awake to watch him sprawled on his back, that defiant mouth now in a slight smile. It was best to face the fact that this would end someday soon, I reasoned. Our age difference wasn't small and now that he knew how much he liked being dominated, he'd want to try it with other women. That's what I told myself as I watched him sleep.

"A twenty-two-year-old? You can't be serious."

My best friend Renee was disgusted. Not just because she was vanilla, although my femdom tastes bothered her too. But to date a parking valet! One I met the night she held her engagement party! She'd wanted me to date the systems analyst from her fiancé's office.

"It's just sex. I told you I was going to do this after Jack moved out."

"You said you were going to play the field," she said. "But I'm only hearing about this kid."

"It's a summer fling. Not a big deal."

Or rather, it was a big deal but a temporary one. It was incontestable that Colton had me under a spell. I dreamt of kissing him until our mouths were feverish and swollen, and then sucking his cock until he came, and rubbing his come all over our mouths until our lips burned. Was that obsessive? Was I losing control? I'd controlled so many men in my time that it was kind of a thrill to succumb to this dizzying, voluptuous ardor that swam through my blood.

"I don't even understand how that all works," Renee went on. "I mean, it's not very dominant of you to suck him off. You're giving him control when you do that."

I laughed. "If that's your experience, you're doing it wrong."

One night I went to the hotel and saw Colton in the lobby talking to a brunette a little older than me. She was in a tennis dress and diamond earrings and cultivating him like her personal hired-help fuck toy. And why wouldn't she? He was delectable. His face was in that dreamy stun of being flattered; he hadn't seen me yet but I was seeing the Colton who was a mystery to me, the Colton who was attracted to other women.

Which of course he was—I knew that logically and I flirted with other men too, but seeing this other him rattled me. A sword of doubt cut through my illusion of possession. He wasn't mine, not really. He belonged to me when he stepped in the house and when the door shut behind him the next day, he was on his own again. I had no idea of his inner complexities, what unpredictable paths he might choose.

The brunette sauntered to the ladies' room, tanned face smug. The thought of her touching him, naked in bed with him, made my stomach curdle. I turned away with self-disgust. I was the ultimate proponent of free love, I reminded myself. I didn't get jealous. I tried to compose myself by the guest-services desk but he found me too soon.

"Where have you been?"

"I'm sick." I'd never lied to him before. But certainly some baffling psychosis had possessed my mind. "I think I'm going to go home."

He frowned. "Do you still want me to come over?"

"No. I'm sorry. I'll call you tomorrow."

I stayed up all night, old horror movies on TV as I squirted Windex on the glass tables and cleaned like a fiend. It had been years since I'd lost sleep over anyone. Who fell in love with a pet? I was shaky and dry-eyed by dawn. He was a very average boy, I reminded myself. Pretty, yes, but there were plenty of beautiful boys to be had in this world. It was ridiculous to get so hung up on what was ultimately a fling.

I had drifted to sleep on the sofa when there was a pounding on the door. I opened it up to Colton looming in the early morning light. "You have someone in there?" he demanded.

"Of course not."

He stormed in, hostile and embarrassed by his vehemence. I made artichoke frittatas. He hadn't been able to sleep either and after doing the dishes, we pulled the drapes, stripped off our clothes and slept all day in each other's arms.

On my refrigerator there was a picture of our trip to Mexico. He was in aviator glasses and leaning against a wooden fence by a burro and his master, dark hair rumpled with suntan oil. His arm was around me, so lanky that he made me look short. I was in a dark-red tank top, my hair bleached a few shades blonder by the sun, and showing that hesitant face I always photographed in, while he looked oddly proud.

The burro's owner was looking sideways at us in a dubious assessment. He knew we were in disguise. I liked this picture because it was the one time someone saw us for the flailing drowners we were. Other strangers—an older couple at dinner, people on the beach—told us we were a beautiful couple. They thought we were lucky. And safe.

My friends decided I had lost my religion over Colton, that dating a twenty-two-year-old parking valet was beneath me. That I was letting it go on for far too long and giving him too much attention.

"You might like him, you know," I said to Renee. "If you can put up with Patrick's bragging and Odette always talking about her horse, I think you can handle a twenty-two-year-old."

And so it happened that one night when Renee and everyone were watching a fight at a sports bar, we stopped in and it didn't go too badly. Everyone in my circle had heard of Colton by this point, and I suspected he lived in their minds as my illiterate sex pet. But now they saw that he was an actual adult, and Renee's fiancé and he got absorbed in a discussion about boxing and it didn't feel that awkward.

"Okay, he's not that bad," Renee said the next night on the phone. "You guys look more—natural together than I would have expected." She paused. "But he is young. And it's just so weird to think of you doing all that kinky stuff."

"Then don't think about it." This was the comment from vanilla people that always irritated me. "Like how I don't think about you having sex or your porn preferences."

"I know. You're right." She exhaled. "So are you bringing him to Odette's party next weekend?"

I hadn't planned on it, but now I saw that it was becoming more unnatural to exclude him. "We'll stop in for a while."

That night at the resort, Colton was nowhere to be found. He wasn't lounging out front with the other valets and he wasn't in the hotel lounge where he usually hung out when I was late picking him up. Annoyed, I walked out back to the employee parking lot. The monsoon's rain still hadn't broken but another dust storm was brewing and a nimbus of amber dimmed the parking-lot lights. The golf course looked like a sepia-tinted photograph. I could feel my long hair getting gritty with the dust and it made me want to push Colton in the dirt, rub dust all through his pretty-boy hair and into his tawny skin.

Then I heard young male voices, one telling a self-important story, the others laughing in contempt. I slid between two SUVs to spy on them: Colton and his friends, all in valet uniforms, drawing leisurely on their cigarettes. The urge to punish him and dominate him and fuck him immediately rolled through me.

I texted him. *I've been out front for twenty minutes.*

He straightened. "Oh fuck...I gotta go." He said his good-byes and hastened toward the hotel. When he got past my SUVs, I slid out and grabbed him by the back of the neck.

He instinctively twisted around to see me; I held him firm and spanked his ass as a rebuke. He winced but he didn't make a sound, as I knew he wouldn't. His valet pals were just fifteen yards away, and I knew exactly how to exploit the situation.

Without a word, I slid my hands down the front of his jeans. The hairy line of his abs, the hardness of his cock thrumming in my hands; I wanted to bite the back of his neck but he was too tall, even in the sandals I was wearing. Instead I marched him through the trees bordering the golf course. The dust-storm air was grittier here from the sand traps. I forced him along the tree line until we were as close as possible to his friends without them seeing us. Two female voices broke the night; other staff had joined them. Colton started to tremble.

I took his pants off first, his hard cock trumping the quiver of his lower lip. His valet shirt came off next. I knew this was his most feverish nightmare and his greatest dream, naked and submissive just a few feet from his coworkers. I scratched his thighs and the soft parts of his stomach, playing with his balls and rubbing his cock until he was visibly choking from the effort to stay silent.

I pushed him to his knees and tied his wrists behind his back with his shirt. He looked up at me and the utter devotion in his eyes stopped me for a moment. He looked exactly like my bound and beautiful young prisoner, and my mouth went dry with a consuming, knee-rattling love for every molecule of his body.

I paused. Then I shook myself out of it, pulled off my shorts and T-shirt and black-lace bra and got on all fours. Reaching through my legs, I spread my pussy open and began fingering myself. I knew this was his favorite view, the one that made him come the fastest, but I also knew Colton couldn't come silently; he always groaned or cried out or made some kind of noise. I looked over my shoulder to see how he was handling this dilemma. He looked tortured and blissful and almost lost, his sweat-damp torso streaked with dust.

We locked eyes and then I backed into him, guiding his cock into my pussy until I felt that delirious flutter of being impaled. A soft grunt escaped Colton. I rocked back and forth on him, my pussy so wet and so swollen I knew I could ejaculate at any second all over him, which would also set him off. He stayed silent but I kept fucking him, subjugating him, driving him deeper into the submissive bliss of being my toy. But it was me who couldn't hold out; a fierce and sudden orgasm bucked through me, so forceful I buried my head in my elbows and bit my arm. I had just become aware of tears on my cheeks when

I felt Colton coming inside me with a raw and broken cry that pierced the night.

We collapsed onto the grass. The night was silent. I didn't know when his friends disappeared, or if they'd heard or seen us. All I could think was that at some point this summer, I had lost control.

How far would it go? We kept pushing, limits disintegrating night after night. I knew I didn't want anyone else. He knew I was his dream come true. The monsoon broke that Friday afternoon, a yellow-purple sky broadcasting thunder and finally, sheets of rain. From my courtyard we watched it drive into the street, oleander petals floating down to the gutter. He was shirtless and handcuffed on my lap as I liberated his cock from his jeans and played with it slowly, keeping him erect without letting him come. A rivulet of rain streaked down between his shoulder blades, over faint welts from my fingernails.

I pushed him into the mud of my courtyard garden, desecrating his torso with flowers and dirt. Anyone walking up to the house would have seen him, naked and groaning as I pulled off his jeans, and I knew the possible exposure was making him throb as he twitched in the dirt. The rain drove into his skin, cleaning him, and I smeared more dirt over his hair, his thighs.

Who do you belong to?

You. Only you.

Inside and into a warm shower we went, kissing each other against the tiles. I wanted to do this forever, desecrating him and cleaning him, ruining him and salvaging him, pulling out every tender secret of his heart.

The neighbors threw a party that night, music thumping across the yards, reminding us of Odette's party that we were supposed to attend. He sat on the floor, leaning against the wall and smoking the cigarette I lit for him. Cuffed hands like the prisoner I made him be. The lamp that we'd knocked off the nightstand was still burning and throwing half the bedroom into shadow. We couldn't look at each other.

The windows were open to the wet night, now that the howling had stopped, now that we were silent with the realization that the body made its own decisions and we were both in service to a force we hadn't intended to find, pulling us toward a vortex of unknown conclusion.

MARYLOU

Lucy Debussy

There were eight sailors who worked in the stokehold. Four ordinary stokers, one chief stoker, one checkman and a petty stokers officer. Marylou was one of the stokers but she called herself Max when she was onboard. She strapped her breasts down with cotton bandages and worked her biceps every evening to keep them hard. She wore short-sleeved shirts to bulk out her form and sometimes she stuffed a single folded sock down the front of her panties. She had dodged her way through the signup by pretending she had a testosterone deficiency that had kept her voice high.

When it came time to go to the bathroom, she would make sure the coast was clear and use the cubicle. Sometimes she had to be patient, and if they were drinking beer in the crew mess her discomfort could last for hours. She regretted slightly that she could not stand next to her coworkers at the urinals because she had great curiosity about their penises. Marylou had always had great curiosity about sailors' bodies. Her father had owned a small, shabby tattoo parlor in a small, shabby port town in the west of Oahu, and she had grown up watching men with chests far too bronzed and big and hard for their faces, clenching their jaws while the needle buzzed over their perspiring skin.

Sometimes when she was folding her uniform at the foot of her bunk, she would catch a glimpse of one of them; a thigh covered in wiry hair, a belly button, a brown flank, a smooth lazy cock. If they were in warmer waters, the men would sleep topless and Marylou would get to see the different bronzes and peaches and browns of their skin on their shoulders and chests.

There was one in particular she liked to look at. He was Romanian and had hair the color of treacle and skin so white it shone like a pebble even in the dark. He spoke perfect English with a perfect English accent. Not like the Dutch sailors who had learned to talk American, or the Indians who spoke with their own inflections. He had impeccable manners. He tipped his hat to ladies in port. He always made sure he was immaculately turned out. She loved, when she had the chance, to watch the attention and care he took when grooming himself, combing his part or cleaning his teeth. His clothes were always folded and pressed as if he had ironed them onto the contours of his body. Marylou imagined that his skin underneath the thick blue twill would be just as immaculate, just as smooth and creamy. She thought up close his body must smell of the same warm cotton soap as his fresh clothing.

The sailors all had a favorite. Marylou would watch in the bar each night as pairs formed off, two by two, as they sipped beer and cracked the shells off monkey nuts. When they got into port they would go in twos and threes to the brothels.

She often wondered what it must be like to be one of the dockside prostitutes, to take so many men at once, men who had so much excitement in them. It would be impossible, she thought, not to be aroused by that quantity of excitement, not to feel it slipping through the red-raw flesh and into the blood, a nourishing pain that had so much promise in it.

They lived in cabins with bunks of four. Marylou slept on the bottom. When it came time to disrobe for bed she usually waited until the men were all asleep or distracted and in she went to the little bathroom. There she would unthread the straps on her breasts, ease them from their bandages, rub the soreness out of them and dress herself in a loose pajama top. Sometimes she found her nipples extra-sensitive from the pressure of being bound down all day, and the light feel of the loose cotton brushing them would be almost unbearable in its delicacy.

The men were all on varying contracts, which meant that the bunk formation was liable to change without notice. Marylou came back from the bathroom one day to find the Romanian boy sitting up in bed, his back to her. She knew it was him because she had looked so many times at the back of his neck. She knew intimately the line where his shoulders centered, where his hair faded into his skin. His back was the color of fresh cream, the disk on the top of a bottle of milk.

Desire shivered like a fish down her body. She felt it low in her belly, the nerves waking up below.

From then on she slept in the bunk underneath him. Every night she would lie, looking up, imagining the shape of his body imprinting on the mattress, trying to see where his weight was falling and the lines of his arms, his back, his thighs, his head. She would close her eyes and picture the way he was reclining with his hand under his cheek, sleep floating the tension away from his body; his muscles, still hurting from lifting and hauling, relaxing slowly.

She would feel a telltale wetness begin to moisten the very

soft tops of her inner thighs. And she would squeeze her legs together, squeezing as much pleasure as she could out of the moment. Then he would turn or shift in his sleep or clear his throat and it would trigger a whole new wave of pleasure in her, like he was moving for her, to make her more comfortable. The other sailors snored on during these silent encounters. She didn't mind their noises, she found them comforting, and she would know then that the way was clear for her to slide her hand down to where the wetness was slowly growing, and gently stroke its barrier along the sensitive lips of her sex. Underneath the seal of liquid they would feel plump and inviting—the warmth of him pressing down from above, the sound of his breathing. She would dip her finger in the wetness like it was an inkwell and gently coax out her bud between two fingers, rubbing it and teasing it and pressing it.

These episodes could last for hours. If she had caught sight of him fresh from the shower that day she would have fuel for her imagination, until in silent, tight, closed ecstasy she would finally come, squeezing her eyes shut, holding on to the rush of breath lest it wake up one of the sleeping men and give her away.

And so Marylou settled into this new rhythm, accepting what she could not have and making the most of what she could.

She was pleasuring herself one night, when she heard a sound, a drawing of breath. She opened her eyes.

From the parallel bunk, a big bronze-armed man called Rafe was staring at her. Rafe was an Englishman, rough-tongued with a brittle London accent, and a gold earring in his ear. He had cropped blond hair and skin so much darker than its natural color from the deck sun that the contrast where the shirtsleeves and the collar ended made him look dipped.

His grizzled chin was propped up on a hand; his eyes were open but languorously relaxed. He had green irises and pig-pink lids; he closed one of them in a slow wink. She looked down, and saw that the covers were off; her trimmed mound was on display, her belly curving down to it, her hand still glistening.

That look haunted her all day in the stokehold. She worked extra hard to tire herself. She shoveled coal that wasn't from her pile and when her oven was full she helped the boy next to her. She ran round the deck six times after her shift, and felt as if the sting in her lungs was punishment for her carelessness. Later on in the crew mess, when all hands were occupied with their bowls of corned beef hash, Marylou looked up, and there it came again, Rafe's languorous wink, promising something, conspiring over some shared secret.

She was careful that night to make sure the cabin was empty before she went into the little bathroom to change for bed. She took her bandages off and slipped on her loose pajama bottoms. When she came out into the cabin Rafe was couched on her bunk, his shoulders hunched into the low space. He too had changed into his sleepwear, drawstring cotton trousers. His chest was bare and Marylou could see the white where the sun hadn't hit, his bulky pectorals, the huge tattoo of the Virgin Mary across his sternum, the dragon on his bicep. He had taken his penis out from his pajama bottoms and was squeezing it at the base. It was huge, shockingly huge, ripe and smooth and crimson at the head, plump as a damson, a pearl shining on its tip. He glanced at Marylou. She stood frozen. Then he dropped it so it bounced a couple of times before hanging firm.

Eight weeks of hunger rushed to her sex, and Marylou suddenly found herself wanting him more than she had wanted anything before or ever would again.

He climbed out from the bunk, his flushed cock still twanging in front of him, and reached behind her back. He pushed his hand down her pajamas, carelessly gripping the flesh of her buttocks. The startle of his touch, his undisguised bestiality, stirred her. She caught her breath as he turned her round by the hips.

He pulled her pajama bottoms down to the ankles and groped until he found the parting underneath her buttocks. His smell came over her shoulder; seawater and an aquatic after-shave. She let him separate the folds of her labia, hold them open with two of his big muscled fingers and slide a third inside her hard enough that she could just feel a strain, a sting and an ache. A second finger joined it. His thumb grazed her clitoris. Pleasure spread down all the way to her toes. He was comfortable playing with a woman.

She forgot the Romanian as he caressed her, one hand in the hair on the back of her head, two of his fingers inside her, rutting back and forth in her slippery juice. Aware of the urgency of time he brought his penis close and took her without ceremony against the wall of the cabin. His forearms braced the wall in front of them and she took great pleasure in digging her nails into the tattoos on them, and thought about all the different women he had brought to orgasm in all the different ports, and it began to excite her, the thought of a promiscuous lover, the cursory animal need of both of them to rub each other to pleasure, no matter whether she liked him or not. His climax was great and hulking, as rough as the stubble on his face. She felt her cheeks grow very hot and came in rocking waves while he was still inside her.

After that, the arrangement had to be maintained. She let him take her whenever he could; on the floor of the shower room, in the cupboard where the engineers' boiler suits were hanging, on quiet corners of the deck at night. She played with herself less and less but sometimes she would catch sight of the Romanian boy—his shoulders bent over his breakfast, his hands tightening a knot—and when she fucked Rafe later that day she would imagine Rafe's huge scarred arms were the Romanian's soft milky ones, his drooping eyelids the Romanian's liquid brown irises.

They were anchored off an island near Fiji when the captain called a day's shore leave. The sun was hot as a griddle, and they paddled ashore in tenders. Marylou's boat was the last and as she approached she could already see that the men had all taken their shirts off and were spread out on the sand like crabs drying for market. Some of them were burnt already.

She found some shade under a tree and looked out at the water, foamy peaks fizzing into hot brown sand leaving tangles of seaweed and crumbs of shell in their wake. From her pocket she took a penknife, found a piece of wood and began to carve idly.

After she had sat for a while, a deep New York accent made her jump. "Now Max, what's a guy like you doing on a day like this with his shirt on. Sun's hot as a pancake, don't you want to get some color?" She looked up to see one of the deckhands, a huge handsome blond man with cruel green eyes, standing above her.

Marylou kept carving away at the little stick of wood. "Don't like the heat."

"You're in the wrong job then ain't you?" He dropped to his haunches. She smelled beer and manly sweet pomade on him. He wiped his sweaty brow with a palm and looked at it.

"You try working the stoke room. Get enough heat in a day. Besides I'm fair, I burn."

"Come on," he had a look in his eye. "What are you hiding under there?"

She could feel the blood creeping up to her face, the neckline of her T-shirt gathering moisture.

"All I'm sayin." He stood up and moved off back down to the shore, shooting her a look over his shoulder.

Marylou looked farther up the beach and saw that three of the bosun's men were kneeling down. The bosun flung a pebble to the ground and the men dropped to their flanks, wrestled their cocks out of their shorts and pushed them into holes dug where the sand met the waterline. They fucked furiously, cursing and swearing at the friction, the grit. The bosun on the starting post laughed hysterically. Marylou watched as each sailor grew red, then beet, then panted wildly. The man in the middle came in a raw, fierce voice, raised both his stocky arms in triumph and collapsed onto the sand. The other men fell headfirst too and they all laughed and wiped the grit out of their eyes.

The sun moved higher in the sky before it began its blinding descent. Some of the sailors looked painfully burnt and took to the sea to cool themselves. Marylou watched the Romanian stand up and walk down to the waterline, and wished she had some salve or ointment she could rub on her palms and smooth across his back. He took off his shorts and tossed them back up where he had left his duffel bag and for the first time Marylou saw his dimpled buttocks, the swing of his slender cock hanging perfectly between his hip bones. It was pink compared to the rest of him, striking against the shiny black curls of hair that ran down all the way from the base of his belly. She felt her blood drop, her nether lips wake up, just looking at him. He turned, and she colored and then looked quickly back down at the carving in her hand, a piece of nothing she was whittling down to the green wood.

They swam and swam while the sun tilted sideways and made crystal the tips on the waves. She saw Rafe looking at her from where he was drinking beer on the sand, and looked around for a patch of trees or shrubbery where they could go.

"Say Max you don't swim?" The blond New Yorker had appeared again.

"Nope."

"Come on, perfect way to cool off."

Marylou flashed a look at Rafe. His lips spread into a great lupine smile, and he rubbed the beer foam off his mouth.

"Say Max," said the New Yorker, "we all think you got something to hide. Bosun's boy says it's a third nipple." He had a raucous look in his eyes that made her uncomfortable. "What about it? Want to play tattoo snap? You've been to Henry's on Oahu haven't you?"

"Got none."

"I don't believe you."

Marylou scratched the back of her neck. "True."

"You need one then. Dimitri," he waved his arm at a big Russian man playing cards near the shore. "He can give 'em. Gives the best. Come on boys, hold him down, let's give him a tattoo." A few of the men began to stir. Marylou shifted. She held tighter onto the knife and spear of carved wood in her hand.

"Just take your shirt off man, you're the only one on the beach who hasn't."

A shadow cut the sun off her legs and she looked up to see Rafe standing over her, rolling a cigarette, a damp swelling pressing against the inside of his cotton shorts. She noticed that two of the bosun's men who had been competing in the sand had drawn closer too, and now their shadows loomed long in front of her, darkening the piece of wood in her hands.

She looked at the four faces, all copper-skinned; all sweating like the men in her father's tattoo parlor. The heat had made them mad, and she suddenly realized exactly why a boy like her would be prime flesh on a day like today.

Marylou felt then not a sense of threat but a sharp feeling of anticipation. That something was going to happen now that she had spent long teenage summer nights wishing and willing for, but which she never really believed could come true, so hadn't bothered to think much about whether she wanted it to or not. She placed her knife and her sharpened stick carefully down on the earth beside her, remembering the day she had first set foot on the ship and how pleased with her reflection in the mirror she had been, starched and proud in her man's uniform.

She sat up and took her burly arms across her chest, and while the four men looked on, peeled her damp white T-shirt off over her head. A big laugh lit up the New Yorker's mouth as he saw the bandages. "What's up with that? Got a tattoo after all Max?"

Marylou breathed in and her torso swelled until it was plain to see the shape of her breasts, even with the hard supporting muscle giving definition to her abdomen below; the gentler curve on top was unmistakably sensuous, unmistakably feminine.

The bosun's men fell silent. The New Yorker took a couple of sarcastic breaths, barely concealing his shock as Marylou felt the perception of her slowly alter. The New Yorker, who was an able-bodied seaman and accustomed to hoicking barrels and ropes and anchors, dropped his neck delicately, as if he was nervous or embarrassed.

Almost shaking, barely controlling her own nerves and excitement, she reached her hand behind her back and began to unfurl her bandages. She unwound herself until her breasts were hanging full and fine, the nipples visibly relaxing and swelling beneath the pattern the cloth had left on them.

For a moment, it didn't seem real. She felt as if she was

watching it happen to someone else. Then one of the New Yorker's hands reached tentatively for her breast; the heat and the damp of it radiating toward her skin. It hovered for a measure of time, then cupped her, tracing the mound with a flat palm, catching her nipple between two fingers, triggering its sensitive release, and an involuntary soft moan from her.

His coarse dirty fingers roamed her flesh, prised apart the skin that stretched across her cleavage. Carefully, he tossed the rest of her bandages into the sand. The power of four sets of eyes watching her was fierce. Marylou felt it even when she closed her eyes. She kept very still while the New Yorker knelt beside her, then ran his hand down her hard flat belly and pushed the waistband of her loose trousers lower and lower, until one finger slipped into the curls of her mound and she heard him gasp, almost a sob, so excited, so pleased he was with what he found.

It was not so much that she knew her fate was sealed as that the infectiousness of their starvation moved her, aroused in her something between maternity—poor bestial slaves to their urges—and vanity. She saw herself reflected in the shine of their eyes, changed at that moment from Max, the runt of the litter, to Marylou, a moon around which planets orbited, fed from her light. Her spine burned. Her flesh shivered under their touches, the hesitant rub of their sandy fingers, as now all four men knelt down to explore each of her limbs, stroking her breasts, tangling her hair, touching her face, her toes, as if they had never seen a woman before; now took a digit into their mouths, now took a lobe of ear or mouthful of neck or inhaled her like she was newfound flowers or clean salt air.

She felt the heat of the whole day seeping out of them. She smelled rum, brandy, beer, soap, linen and seaweed.

She closed her eyes and stopped thinking of them stoking,

showering, shoveling fish and potatoes into their mouths, and instead stretched in the hot sand, felt the coolness of the palm shade above her and the drift of seashore wind, felt now a thick finger stirring her juice, whose she didn't care, and now another, pushing her wider. And now her trousers and shorts had been slipped down her legs and off by two or more hands, and soon her own hands were reaching out, finding coarse resistance in patches of curled hair, soft wet skin, scents from different parts of them, sweet shampoo, cool soap, warm breath, cigarettes. She felt fingers massage the sand from between her toes, hot tongues clean her stomach and shoulders. She reached out and probed a navel, kissed a sweet stubbly moving mouth. She reveled in being the well from which thirsty sailors drank like madmen, stroking her, pushing her, stretching her, causing her to ache.

She opened her eyes to see the New Yorker had slipped between her legs. His hot brown nipples were grazing her breasts; his cock drove hard inside her wetness. Above, she felt the contrasting softness of Rafe's hands in her hair. From down the beach other sailors had drifted closer, curious, and now the orgy was spreading, trousers were being lowered, penises dug out and fondled and shared, open mouths touching. She saw from under the hoods of her lids two of the other stokers grab each other with such fervor it sent a fresh shock of pleasure down her. She arched her back, prising her limbs into the ground like a sea creature, opening her lips, her mouth, her sex, making herself available, pushing her left nipple closer to a man's tongue, hearing the scale of pleasure trickle up his voice as she took his balls between her fingers, poked asscheeks open with her toes, rocked in the rhythm with which the blond New Yorker fucked her.

She heard Scandinavian accents, French accents, Russian curses, American shouts. Her eyes closed, her mind traveled their faces, journeyed their excitement, their fevered desires. She thought of their fetishes, the places they had sailed to, their first kisses, tender and tentative, repressed under years of thickened personality and sea work.

Marylou thought that now she must know what it felt like to be one of the dockside whores confronted with such depraved lust, such swollen, bursting mouths that could bruise with their impatience. She opened her eyes.

Her beautiful Romanian was lifting one of her feet, kissing the ball of her ankle. His brown eyes were closed, his lashes long and black, his hands as reverent as they were when he prepared a knot, or carried letters he had written home to the purser's office, or ran along the surface of the mouth organ he sometimes played. His cock was darker now, long and engorged and pointing skyward.

Now, she thought, watching him, *now as they take their pleasure, I will take mine.*

REALITY TV

Alyssa Turner

"Are you spending another evening in that window, Marcella?" Abby only sounds annoyed as she asks me the same rhetorical question I've heard every night this week. Her keys clank on the table next to the door, and I glance in her direction.

"Okay, so I'm nosy. Beats watching TV since they cut off the cable."

"Maybe if you'd paid the bill instead of getting a new set of headshots…" she says, taking off her sneakers.

I pout. "You don't mean that."

And she relents. "No, *chica*. I don't. You know I don't." Abby kisses me on the cheek. "So what's playing tonight on NYC live, Amsterdam and One Hundred and Twenty-Third Street edition?"

"Checked out a girl doing Pilates over the bodega."

"Big deal, I can see that working at the gym any time of the day."

"Oh, but she was only wearing her panties." I turn to her and smile.

Abby isn't convinced. "Give me those," she says with a devilish grin and snatches the binoculars out of my hands before I can protest. "Now let's see here. It was the third window from the left, wasn't it?"

"Wasn't what?" I act clueless, but I won't win any Academy Awards with my performance.

"Uh-huh, just like I thought." She peers down at me from over the Nikons I scored for a bargain at a pawnshop in Times Square. "Same dude we caught stroking his dick in front of the TV three nights ago."

I'm red, I know it. "Really, I didn't see him."

"Guilty little Marcella, can't tell a lie for shit." She's laughing at me.

"Stop it." I can't help it. I'm giggling with her.

She takes another look at the nameless guy sitting naked on his couch with just one light on in the kitchen and the blue flickering glow of the television washing his taut body. "You've been watching him every night, haven't you?"

"Maybe I have." I shrug my shoulders.

Abby cocks her head to the side with an eyebrow raised and returns the binoculars to her eyes. "Where's the zoom on these things?" I start to show her, but she waves me away. "Never mind, I got it."

"Trying to get a closer look?"

"Not at his cock, Marcella. You know I only like pussy, baby." She winks at me. "I only like your pussy, to be exact." Then, looking again, she continues, "No, I think this guy looks familiar."

"Get out of here."

"No really, I think this dude takes my climbing class."

"Let me see," I say, and she hands the binoculars back to me. "I don't recognize him."

"He comes to my last class on Fridays. You're busy exploiting thirsty stockbrokers for tips by then."

I turn to her with a frown, but Abby has a look in her eye that makes my blood pump straight to my pussy.

She puts down the Nikons and slides her hand flat against the front of my tank top and slips her fingers into my yoga pants. "Maybe you should try to make it tomorrow evening. Anything that gets you this wet is something I want to be a part of."

"You're not jealous?"

Abby brushes her lips against mine as her fingers weave their way into my slickened folds. "Baby, don't I always get you whatever you want?"

"Yes."

"You want chocolate cake, I go to the bakery. You want a bubble bath, I run the water." She rolls her tongue against mine in a single slow wave. "You have a taste for some cock?" Her voice is throaty. "I'll see what we can do about that, too."

"I love you." All I want to do is show her how much. But Abby is scooting off to our bedroom.

"Stay there. I'll be right back." I hear her rustling in the night table. "Don't you move."

Sliding down my pants, I'm ready and waiting for her when she returns. Abby saunters back in peeling off her T-shirt and dropping it to the floor. In her other hand, a strap-on harness dangles between three fingers. "Hurry up and bend over before he finishes," she says, and I do as I'm told. Looking through the binoculars, I'm pleased to see we're not too late. "You keep watching him stroke his cock. and I'll help you imagine what he feels like."

"But you fuck like a girl." I tease her with a wide grin and my eager booty wiggling in anticipation, waiting while she fastens my favorite dildo snug against her boy shorts.

"Oh, is that right?" Abby squares herself behind me and wraps her tawny fingers onto my hips. She takes a nice firm hold of my sandy brown ponytail and makes sure I know that she intends for me to eat my words. "Well, let's see if you scream like one."

She pops her hips forward and the slickened silicone passes into me with ease as I pick up my view of our neighbor quietly loving himself across the avenue. Neither of us have a doubt in the world how this will turn out. Me, calling her name and clawing at the curtains while she whips that silicone dick and strums my clit like an acoustic guitar.

Abby fucks like a girl all right—one that knows exactly where to find my sweet spot. She holds me tight, keeping me steady on my elbows as the pretty picture of his cock sliding in and out of his fist bounces in my hands. And then he's coming, his shoulders hunching forward with a stutter. Too far for me to see him overflow, but my mouth hangs open just wishing for a taste. Abby whispers in my ear, "Tomorrow, baby. He's gonna love you."

"How are you so sure?" I breathe through a moan.

Abby only laughs lightly though my hair. "My sweet Marcella, I know."

All week, I can't wait until class. Now he's not a couple of hundred feet away. He's so close I could touch him.

"Hey, you're pretty good." My recent obsession has a voice, a deep relaxed Brooklyn flavor rounding his syllables. I nod at him as he dangles next to me twenty-five feet in the air.

"I have a really good teacher."

"Yeah, Abby is pretty badass." He tries not to be obvious, but I can tell he's checking me out, his eyes lingering just a few seconds on the way my ass looks hanging out of my harness. I follow his gaze and he looks away.

I dig my toe into a hold and leverage myself farther up the wall. "It's okay, my girlfriend is always saying my ass looks great suspended above her."

He doesn't skip a beat, following me higher. "Your girlfriend?"

"Abby." I wave down at her, and she waves back.

He looks down and then back at me. "She's right. Lucky woman."

"Her or me?"

"Both, I guess."

"I'm Marcella."

"Brett. I'd shake but my hands are a bit occupied at the moment." His smile is a good substitute. "I've never seen you in class before."

"I'm usually at work, but Abby insisted I call out sick today."

"Oh yeah, why?"

"I'll let her tell you." With that I tug on my safety rope and start repelling down to Abby, who's been watching our interaction from below.

Brett follows, curiosity thinly disguised on his face.

It's the end of class and the rest of the students are making their departures. Brett thanks his spotter and lingers, stretching his muscular arms behind his back.

"Plenty loosened up now, Brett?" Abby asks him.

"I feel like I'm just getting started." He tilts his head. "What, do you have some kinda tricked-out new route to put me up against?"

"Something like that...if you're up for it." Abby sidles up next to me and slides her hand over my ass. "I see you've met my Marcella."

I can't help the way my tongue is dancing across my bottom

lip. Abby has started running laps around my asscheek with her finger.

"Yeah, we met." Brett seems to know there's more to that statement. He taps his heel a few times and shifts his weight. I can see the vein in his neck swell as he swallows.

"She's a handful—a real firecracker if you give her a chance to warm up," Abby continues, drawing things out further. Even I'm starting to get anxious.

"I can see how that could be true," Brett says, smiling in my direction.

"What if I told you that sometimes I could use some help... with her?"

Brett shifts his weight just slightly, tipping his head with a measure of disbelief. "You're fucking with me, right?"

Abby smiles at him like a dragon about to shock and awe. "Brett, I think you know by now that in this gym, it's all about the work. I don't play around."

He returns her surly stare with his own. I notice how his eyes look suddenly smoky in the intensity of the moment. Abby can make things get serious in a heartbeat. She has that way about her that tells everyone she lives in a no bullshit zone. She's smirking now. "See this is my problem. Marcella thinks I fuck like a girl."

"Abby!" I can't believe how she blurted that out.

Abby folds her arms. "Do you want to help her make a comparison?"

"Oh my god!" I gasp, hiding behind my hands.

Abby plows forward despite my mortification. "This is the last class tonight. I can lock the door."

Brett doesn't look shocked. Even if he is, he's way too cool for that. He looks amused. "You want me to do your girlfriend. Right here."

"Do you want to...do my girlfriend?" Abby sweeps her hand across my shoulder and guides my ponytail away from my neck. She's nibbling in the spot that makes me giggle. Only I'm not giggling. I open my mouth and exhale the breath I've been holding in one long shaky moan.

"Does she want to?" he asks, and I suddenly realize that I haven't said anything to make him know that this isn't just her idea.

I've been frozen in place, watching them discuss the matter. It takes a gentle squeeze of my ass from Marcella to encourage me to speak my mind. "I, uh...think you're pretty sexy." One foot in front of the other and I'm standing directly in front of him. "Yeah, I want to." My hand floats to the emblem on his chest and traces the outline of the FDNY Maltese cross printed there. His chest is firm under my touch, and he doesn't move away. I can't wait to see him naked, up close and in person. But I need to come clean first. "We live across the street from you...and you leave the shades up a lot."

Brett looks at me quizzically. I watch his face change as he settles on a response. "You've been watching me, huh? Watching me do what?"

I know I can say it. Abby tilts her head, and her eyes are narrow on me like a spear. "I watch you jerk off."

He presses his lips together and nods slowly, his expression disarmingly placid. "And you want to give me something to think about for the next time."

I shrug, losing my voice again.

Abby slaps my ass. "You tell him what you want, *chica*."

"I want...to see it."

There's a simmering smirk on his face now, as he removes his gloves. "What do I get to see?"

Abby slips her arms around me from behind and pinches my

nipples through my sports tank. "Just let me lock the door."

She leaves me standing there, still feeling the electricity she sparked running across my chest. He's watching me keenly, pulling slowly at the strings that affix his shorts to his waist. I stand there acquainting my teeth with the flesh of my bottom lip.

I sense Abby returning and turn to watch what she will do; her dark hair is now free from the bandana she'd been wearing. It falls seductively in her face, her eyes looking feral, her hips swaying with saucy confidence as she approaches. She doesn't hesitate. She reaches for my cheeks and plants her mouth squarely on mine in mid-step. Then she crosses between us and grabs the folding chair in the corner of the gym. I can't stop my cheeks from burning, already guessing what she has planned.

When Abby takes a seat, she does so with languid grace. Her back is stretched proud, her long neck squaring her head firmly in place. All so her eyes can burn straight to my core. She pats her lap two times in a quick repeat. I take a hesitant step and she smiles.

"Come here, *chica.*"

Brett is watching this dance play out between us. His lip twitches just slightly as I sashay toward my girlfriend. It's not just her wanton glare that has heat prickling up my spine. Brett is just as invested in what will come next, and I love the way he's licking his chops.

The chair is front and center and Abby reaches her hand out to my hip, guiding me with little effort to lie across her lap. I feel like a rag doll, my arms dangling toward the floor as I struggle to keep an eye on Brett. Abby's hand eases into my crotch, toying with my clit through the thin Lycra fabric of my shorts. My mouth falls open at the sensation. My eyes widen at the sight of Brett's thick cock sliding in his hand.

Abby peels the elastic band down my ass, and her fingers

sample the evidence of my hunger. "Sweet Marcella," she whispers in my ear and presses into me slowly, then pulls out to show me what she's found. I love the way her fingers glisten. Next she will have a taste, she always does.

A low rumble erupts out of Brett when her fingers reach her mouth. I watch the satisfaction dawn on Abby's face as she sucks every drop. My ass wiggles with a silent request and her fingers are in me once again, and again, and again.

It's not enough that she's pumping me so fast I can't keep the moans from flying free from my lips; Brett's beautiful cock has me locked into a singular thought, looping in everlasting redundancy. *Fuck me.*

"What did you say, *chica?*"

Have I said that out loud? I take a breath and stare directly at him. "I want you to fuck me."

Brett's hands are on me in less than a flash. He looks at me with a critical eye, judging my reaction. No one could blame him for questioning if this is for real. I hardly believe it myself. But my patience is running thin and my pussy is begging to know if he feels as good as he looks. "I want it."

Abby fishes in her pocket. "Give my baby what she wants, Brett."

He takes the condom, ripping the foil with his teeth and rushing it onto his shaft. Taking a handful of my shorts and tearing them farther down my legs, he's right where I want him.

Abby caresses my cheek with the back of her fingers and then pulls the hem of my shirt up to ensure it isn't in the way of her view. Her feathery strokes dance up and down my spine, and the anticipation is taking me to another planet.

But the way Brett takes possession of my hips brings me back. He's here, now, ready to enter me with the cock I've coveted from afar. The pure notion, the mere idea is more than I could have wished for. Abby's gift is poised behind me, ready to be just the amount of fantasy I need, just the right amount of man to satisfy my craving, my derelict desire. His fingers are daggers in my flesh, searing-hot pinches that are going to leave a mark. This won't resemble the uncertain fumbling of an overanxious college sophomore. I think Brett means to make a lasting impression on my body.

It's not just the way his cock eases past my shorts and laps at my pussy that's making me whimper. It's the look on Abby's face as he does that has me sucking down a shaky breath. Even as he presses forward, filling me with the delicious pairing of his rugged need and sinuous flow, I am captivated by the words on Abby's lips. "Mmm...*chica*, you like that, don't you?"

She wraps her fist with my tank top, cinching it against my skin like a harness. Her grip on me is strong, and she knows it. "You didn't answer me."

"I...ahh..." I can't seem to form the words.

Brett bottoms out within my cunt. His thighs are hot against mine as he remains there, lingering in place, still like a threat. "Speak, Marcella," he says with a firmness that curls my toes inside my sneakers.

"It's good, so good," I croak.

He seems satisfied with my answer and pounds the sentiment home, the rest popping from my open mouth with each beat of his hips against my ass. "So—good—oh—my—god."

Maybe it's the slip-slide of him, hot like lava flowing in and out of me, that is making me moan his name. A real live boy is so much hotter than a dildo, no matter how perfectly selected for my pleasure it is. Brett squeezes my hips and rakes his pelvis against my ass as he dives deeper than he has before. I feel absorbed by him, melting around his cock as it thumps with arousal inside of me. He blows out a long soft breath, tickling my ear. "Sweet."

Abby kisses my forehead. "Yes you are, *chica*. Very sweet." She taps me at the base of my spine three times in quick procession. "Up now. I want to lick you."

Brett eases away on Abby's request without a measure of complaint. The look on his face is expectant, but not demanding. It's clear to both of us that this is Abby's game. She's the one making the rules.

All I have to do is stand; she puts me where she wants me. Against the rock wall, arms high, catching holds in my grip, I catch a glimpse of her over my shoulder before she lowers herself to her knees. It's the look on her face that makes me prop my ass up. She looks hungry. Her hands are between my thighs, opening my legs like she's parting a curtain. We're onstage all right. Brett is fixated, sitting now in the chair next to us with his cock gleaming in his fist. It makes me wetter to see my juices on him, to know that Abby has shared some of her goodies with him.

Then her tongue finds its way between my folds with a flat needy lap of my slit. I hear her sigh with a gritty rasp at the tail. My stomach does a flip-flop and she returns to the place she finds so tasty. It's all cool air and hot caresses down there as she lathers my clit with her tongue. My pussy clenches with the need to be filled. Abby gives me her finger, and I whimper.

"You want more?" She adds a third finger and twists them like a corkscrew. "You want his fat cock again?"

"Yes." For her information I'll make sure she knows how much. "Please, Abby. Let me have it."

Abby slides herself underneath me, propping her head against the rock wall and draping her arms around my hips. She speaks, though not to me. "What are you waiting for?"

I can hear him huff a chopped snicker. "Say no more." His large hands are on me in mere seconds. I intentionally don't look, wanting to be surprised by the moment he will take me again...borrow me again.

He rakes my cheeks apart, lifting them, looking. Abby also has a perfect view of my slit as he presses into it. Only I am left in the dark, my eyes closed shut tight. *Shhhiittt.* My brain is trying to remember to breathe when she lands her tongue on my clit and slides it forward to where Brett's cock is buried inside me.

This is more than I'd asked for. This is the apex of pleasure, the best of both.

My fingernails scratch against the resin holds as I beg them to keep me upright. Legs trembling, sweat beading on my brow, though my real workout has ended with the oddest cooldown I've ever experienced. Brett is just getting started. His body is pressed against mine, blanketing me in his masculine scent while his cock makes acquaintance with my deepest recesses. Abby's busy mouth on my clit reveals her concentration. This is for me, all for me. I wanted dick, and she provided. I can only thank her by coming, hard, with a deluge of gratitude and love.

When it is time, Abby knows it. Maybe it's the sound of my moans, climbing an octave for every new thrust. This is her cue. "Give her to me," she demands and Brett pulls out, leaving me to pour my orgasm into Abby's open mouth. As my insides crash together, Brett's warm wet streaks crisscross my ass and scurry down the back of my thigh.

"There now, *bella chica.*" Abby pats her hand against my pussy and it splashes like a rain puddle. "You get what you wanted?"

I can't help but smile at Brett over my shoulder. "You were even better than I imagined."

He takes the compliment with a shrug. "Any time you want me, Marcella. I'll be there live and in person."

Abby pulls me down to the mat, and I curl into her open arms. She tosses him his pants. "Just don't go installing shades. You're Marcella's favorite show."

He laughs at that and fixes the drawstring on his warm-ups. "Same time next week?"

Abby nods and kisses my temple. "Don't be late. I got a new course planned." The wink of her eye makes me wonder if I'll need another excuse to get out of bartending. "It should be a hell of a workout."

GENTLEMAN'S VALET

Sommer Marsden

My first thought was that it was ugly.

"I see that look," George said. "I know that look."

"Oh really?" I circled what was possibly the world's ugliest chair. "What do I know? Antiques are your deal. Not mine."

"Do you know what it is?"

"An…um…torture device?"

I couldn't help but laugh as I ran my hand over the small wooden shelf at the top. Where a person's head would normally be if he were seated in a normal chair was this little ledge with a groove. Below that hung a wooden hanger on a hook and then lower down was the seat itself. George moved past me and lifted the seat to reveal a space inside.

"This is a Gentleman's Valet."

"I thought that was a person," I teased, touching the wooden hanger on the hook just to watch it swing.

"If there's wealth involved it can be. But in the workingman's case, even a mildly well-to-do man's, it's this chair."

George took my hand in his much bigger one and ran my fingers over the smooth grooved shelf.

"This is for your tie clips. Your cuff links. Your change. Your lighter…"

His lips kissed the back of my neck, and I almost shivered.

"This is where you can hang your shirt." He touched the wooden hanger. "Maybe your jacket. Drape your tie around it."

His fingers trailed down the nape of my neck, tracing a fine line of sparks along the curve of my shoulder.

"Oh," I managed.

He indicated the seat. "This is where a man could keep anything else he needed. Maybe a pair of socks. His wallet. Keys. Or just anything he wanted to keep stashed."

He bent over, tugging my hand so I bent too. He put his hand in the compartment. I put my hand in the compartment. As I mimicked him, his free hand caressed the swell of my ass.

"Or maybe," George went on, "his girly magazines."

I smiled.

"Condoms. Handcuffs…" His hand caressed my ass again. "A paddle."

I tried not to react in any way that would give away the rampant arousal coursing through me.

"You think?" I said.

"I have plans for this little beauty," he said. His hand made another territorial sweep of my ass, and I wondered if he meant the chair or me.

"Yes? What's that?"

"Go take off your dress, Jess."

I laughed because it rhymed.

"I'm not kidding. Go get undressed and come back here to me. I've had this chair for two weeks in the garage."

"And you only brought it in here today because…" I realized I was holding my breath.

"Because I have today off and have shut off my phone. I have you and this chair and we're alone." He tapped my bottom with a stiff hand. "I won't ask again. Go take off your dress."

I hurried away. My legs felt as if they were going to buckle on me in the next heartbeat. Or maybe the one after that.

I took off my dress and since that was all I'd been instructed to do, I returned to him in my hose, my heels, my bra and my panties. I was thankful to the gods of serendipity that everything was pretty and matched. I wasn't stuck in a decrepit bra or ugly knickers or snarled hosiery.

"Good girl. I was wondering if you'd arrive bare-assed naked or only missing the item specified." He clapped softly. "Bravo."

I was wet between the legs, light in the head. So, I said the only thing I could think to say. "How would you like me?"

He cocked his head and studied me. "I think that first I'd like you to grab the small cuff-link shelf. But remember, don't put too much weight on it or you'll bend it. This lovely thing is in pristine condition."

When he said that I knew I was in trouble. A thought that made my heart beat faster and my head spin a little. I put my hands, the left laid neatly atop the right, on the small wooden shelf. I made sure to put barely any weight on it at all. Which, when I bent forward a bit, put all the stress on my lower back and ass. His hands slid down the small of my back, cupped my butt. He found the wet center of me and drove a finger against it. Which only served to wedge my wet panties to my soaked slit.

I bit my lip and waited.

"I think I'd like to see you keep your composure as I use the paddle. Doesn't that sound fun?"

I nodded.

He tapped me once. Hard.

"Yes, Sir," I amended.

"Let me just reach around here into the handy dandy cubby and grab that paddle."

He must have filled it while I was taking off my dress. I had no idea what that compartment held. He pressed his hard cock to the back of me as he reached past me. He was still wearing trousers but the feel of it elicited a sharp inhalation from me.

The paddle said BAD in red leather letters. "I'm going for a look here. More cherry red than cherry-blossom pink. I'll paddle you till I'm satisfied. So, take a big breath, Jess."

I obeyed, sucking air deep into my lungs before pressing my ass back in an act of true submission. The paddle whacked against me with a cheerfully dull thud. My body jerked as a thick pain filled me. A dull pain as opposed to the sharp sting of an open hand. It was an act of utter concentration. Focusing on not putting too much pressure on the cuff-link tray, not leaning on it hard enough to bend the slender metalwork that held it above the hanger.

"You're doing remarkably well. I can see you are being very aware of my treasure, here." Three more thick blows landed on my ass. Inside my panties, I was terribly wet. I could feel the warm slide of my juices as he continued to paddle me. I could only let myself be aware of it for a split second at a time, or I would lean too heavily on the wooden shelf.

When I had chewed my lower lip swollen with concentration, George stopped. The leather paddle hit the floor, and I heard his zipper. He stepped out of his trousers slowly as blood beat slug-gishly beneath my paddle-reddened cheeks. Heat and pain and viscous pleasure occupied my mind.

I started when he shoved my panties down, making sure to

preserve my thigh-high stockings. His fingers slipped inside of me with ease, and I blushed.

"Drenched. I'm glad you enjoyed that as much as I did."

I nodded. "I did, Sir."

"Reach under there and you'll find two alligator clips."

I didn't react outwardly, but inside I trembled. I hated them. Hated that dull chewing pain on my skin. But when they were removed, it was nearly transcendental. The pleasure-pain of fresh rushes of blood traveling to the tortured spot was heart stopping.

I lifted the leatherette seat and found them without looking. They were lined up at the very front where I would feel their small metal presence.

"Hand them over."

I turned and put them in his hand.

"Face me all the way, Jess."

I turned and watched him calmly pop the front of my bra open and push it off. He opened the clamp and let me see the ragged teeth. "Please keep your eyes on what I'm doing. No looking away."

George brushed the metal over my nipple until the coolness of it raised the flesh up into a tight pink knot. Then he slowly let the jaws shut on my tender flesh. I blew out a breath when I realized I wasn't breathing.

He smiled, nodded, leaned in and kissed me gently. His tongue slipped along my lower lip and then slid into my mouth. The kiss was gentle. Accented by the sharp bite of the other clip on my right breast as he applied it. He stepped back, surveyed his work and smiled.

"On your knees now, Jess. Face the gentleman's valet. Hold the ends of the wooden hanger and put your ass out. We've gotten it cherry red but I'm itching to feel my bare hand on that warm skin."

I thought ten strokes. He liked things even. I could handle the clamps for ten strokes. Ten wasn't so bad.... I tried to convince myself of this as he began. The first bare-handed blow landed on my already welted skin, and I jumped. The pain shot through me, rattling me as the sensation of the blow augmented my awareness of the tiny metal jaws on my nipples.

But through it all, lust and need burned warm and sweet in my belly.

Every blow rocked me, and every rock made me clutch at the smooth wood in front of me. Again, I had to focus on not pulling too hard on his precious find. It was most likely, judging by its appearance, older than the two of us put together. The wood my hands warmed as I clutched it smelled like cedar. I lost myself in that rich cedar scent as blow ten shot fire down my flanks.

With every heartbeat my cunt constricted. Little spasms of hot pleasure that had me chewing my lower lip again. In my mind he lost his edge, lost his cool, lost his calm exterior. Dropped to his knees. Fucked me hard enough to ram my belly against the lip of the lovely leatherette seat. Fucked me hard enough to make the liftable seat flap restlessly, making a banging sound that would remind me, I was sure, of the sound of one hand clapping.

I shook my head, fighting off the crazy thoughts that filled me as I realized blow eleven had landed. It was the first strike that truly provoked a noise from me.

"You were expecting ten," he chuckled. It wasn't a question. I nodded. "Yes, Sir."

"Today I figured I'd go for a baker's dozen."

With that, two more blows crashed down, and I found myself trying to ram my clit against the edge of the seat. Only it didn't line up. I was humping air.

"Oh, poor Jess," he said. "Turn around and face me. But stay on your knees."

I spun to face him, my knees screaming—a totally different flavor of pain from my ass, which was a totally different flavor than my aching nipples.

He ran the tip of his cock along my upper lip as if painting me with lipstick. I kept my tongue in my mouth and did nothing until instructed. When he brushed the hair back from my brow and said, "Open," I opened so fast my mouth made a soft popping sound.

He chuckled. "You really are such a good girl. You please me more often than not. And even when you don't please me," he said, winking, as if sharing a great secret, "I love you."

Pleasure saturated my nerve endings and my pussy seemed to grow thicker, plumper and even more desperate for him to enter me. It was all I could think of. Him filling me with his big hard cock. Him rocking his hips and kissing me until I came. Him eating up my cries like the small, sweet things they were.

With that he was holding the sides of my head and fucking my mouth. Not slow and gentle, but with great eager strokes that meant he was taking from me what he needed, and that made me happy beyond measure.

There came a point where he hung his head and swore softly, then offered me his hand chivalrously. I took it, stood and looked down at my heels until he put a finger under my chin and tilted my face up so I'd look at him.

Keeping that gaze, he took one alligator clip off. I gasped and he leaned in to kiss me. A moan overcame me as the blood that had been denied that constricted flesh began to flow again. It was the most exquisitely pleasant pain.

George leaned in and licked my nipple. When I hissed, he sucked it. A gush of wetness escaped me, and my hips thrust forward on their own. He put his hands on my hip bones and sucked again. I sighed.

The second clamp came off, and a sob slipped out of me. It went from a quiet sob to a consuming one as he settled his mouth on that fragile halo of flesh.

George thrust thick fingers into me, holding me around the waist as he did it. "You did very well, sweetheart," he said.

That alone caused my pleasure to swell.

He thrust harder, making sure to drive the knuckle of his thumb against my throbbing clitoris. I rarely came from fingers alone but the paces he'd put me through before this had primed me. I was well past ready, far down the road from juicy. I was on the breathtaking cusp of coming before he'd even touched me. When he thrust roughly and truly knocked my clit with that knuckle, I sagged in his arms.

I said one word, remembering myself at the very last second. "Sir."

"I'm not sure, Jess, if it's this pristine piece or how well you did, or a combination of your beauty and its, but I think I've lost my resolve."

I waited, biting the very tip of my tongue. I held it there between my teeth because all of me was shaking. Even my jaw.

"Put that sweet lush ass on the edge of the seat, please." He jacked his cock in one hand as he said it. "Be careful not to put your head against the hanger or the wooden tray. We want to keep this as pristine as possible."

I balanced there, thighs spread, cunt wet, on the very edge of the leatherette seat. I was not a gentleman putting on my socks and garters. I was not a man having a seat to put on my wristwatch or cufflinks. I was his whore, precariously perched on his new treasured items, pussy drenched, thighs splayed, heart racing.

It was perfect.

George knelt. "Do you like the irony, Jessica? Me on my knees?"

I just stared. At his almost severe mouth. The way it turned more pliable and welcoming when he gave me a wry smile.

"Turns out you've pleased me too much for me to tease you any more. Kudos."

He wrapped my leg around his waist, found my slick split with his cockhead. He dragged that velveteen skin along my wetness until I mewled softly. I wasn't proud of that sound but it was how I felt in a nutshell. Eager. Willing.

He moved into me and I gripped the edge of the seat, willing myself not to move. He wanted to take me, and my job was to be taken. I concentrated on holding my body still, letting him tilt me and bend me and fuck me at his will. He smiled, knowing the lengths of my control. When we fucked "normally" I moved and clutched and thrust and groaned. Now I simply held my body taut, at the mercy of his will and my shredding amount of control.

"You impress me, Jess. You've yet to come undone."

He hiked my leg a bit higher, thrusting into me so forcefully the vintage chair had a good case of the tremors. I gripped the lip of the seat, held my breath until he pushed his thumb past my lips and I did what he expected. I sucked.

A shiver skittered through him before he could suppress it and deep in that secret place inside of me that remained bright and alert and willful during these interludes I felt victorious.

"Damn," he laughed. The amused sound of a man bested.

He thrust harder and the chair squealed. He chuckled, his fingers biting into the meat of my hip as I continued to languidly suck his thumb like it was his cock.

He leaned forward, the root of his cock bumping my clit so precisely I gasped.

"You may," he said. Then he moaned and the sound alone pushed me forcefully past my invisible line of self-control. I came with a cry, my cunt milking him.

"Jesus," he groaned. "Your perfect velvet pussy," he laughed. Again he sounded bested and my heart swelled.

"What do you think of my treasure?" he asked, fixing my hair. It had swung in tatters and tangles around my face. He held my thighs in his hands, his cock still buried inside me though softening.

"I like it." I smiled.

"I like it too. I like it even more now."

"Me, too."

When he stood he offered me a hand. I took it. He kissed my knuckles, my palm, my throat. "Now put all our toys inside the seat. I'll move it upstairs once you're done. I think I've found the perfect third party to our games. Every gentleman needs two things."

"What are those?" I asked.

He pinched my nipple playfully. "A beautiful woman and a way to organize her undoing."

CHRYSALIS

Nikki Adams

This morning, just as the elevator closed, I caught the faint trace of perfume. Whisper of a delicate flower, soft as pillows and sighs. Jasmine, perhaps. It teased like a smile from the far side of a room, and I fell headlong into thoughts of a pencil skirt, and heels clicking across a tiled floor. Who those things belonged to didn't entirely matter. It was a spark, and the spark was what mattered.

Jasmine-scented spark.

Once the doors opened, I was busy—always so busy. Another day playing the role of a coldhearted bitch who was too engaged to waste time—too occupied to fuck around. Double-checking facts, coordinating with clients, researching relevant cases and, when the other side refused to settle, going to court. And when in court, owning it. Head high, shoulders relaxed, walking with purpose and engaging the jurors with my eyes. Suggesting to them just what it was they should think. Twenty-six of my clients had walked away with at least a million, often much more. Well, not all of them walked—some while away their lives with multiple prosthetics, wheelchairs, hospital beds or machines that have become the most unwanted of friends. Sometimes, winning is nothing at all.

Busy-busy-busy. Very good money, but so little time.

Still, on evenings like this, I'm carried elsewhere. Heat moves to the forefront, and my desire for another woman becomes unbearable. I start to swelter. Burn.

Sparks, like the one from the elevator, become smolder when I see a jogger with her mouth slightly open, ponytail swaying, lower back shimmering with perspiration. I imagine kissing her there, welcoming the salty-sweetness lingering upon her skin. I plunge into fantasies of the two of us tangled, panting and wet with exertion. When the smolder bursts to flame, I reach for the phone. The service I use is discreet, and the girls are young and perky. Earlobes, necks and nipples; fingernails, thighs and clits. I get what I need, I tip generously when we both get off, and she goes away.

My heart is strictly off limits, and I always sleep alone. Always. It has worked out pretty well for me, because I just don't have time to fuck around.

Lately, though, it's all turned lackluster. A pulling has risen, leaving me hungry for more than another call girl feigning niceties to squeeze out a bonus. And I surely don't want to waste time chasing down and bedding an inquisitive straight chick, then watch her fall apart at the seams just because I make her come.

No.

I need someone to move me out of myself and into an intensity I haven't known before. I want someone to thoroughly intoxicate me—be my drug.

* * *

While perusing the W4W section, a posting caught my eye:
A different kind of woman...
Zhanna, 28, 5'10", M2F Non-op.
I went through the picture links. She was cute. Very cute.
Casting a look over her shoulder, she showed a very faint lump
in an otherwise womanly neck. Another photo revealed blonde
hair reaching her lower back. Her arms were slender. Little
breasts pushed against a designer T-shirt, and she had an ass that
begged to be patted. Black stilettos accentuated long legs.

Well, damn.

I scanned her profile again. *M2F Non-op.* For whatever
reason, she'd decided to keep what she had.

How long since I had been with a man, I wondered? Brad
was the last, and that was four years ago—perhaps five. Either
way, it hadn't been long enough for me to particularly miss it. I
supposed it wasn't his fault that he was so darn clumsy, though
the experience was similar with those I'd had with the other
men I'd known. They just fumbled around down there. But a
female—particularly when intent on pleasure—knows exactly
what to do. Women understand what women want.

So why her? What was it about this woman that piqued my
interest? She wasn't a female in the Merriam-Webster sense. At
the same time, she surely wasn't a man either. No, she was a
woman—a female who happened to have something different.
She was that tiny sliver in a rainbow, the misty mingling of two
hues.

And she was looking to spend her quiet time with a
woman....

The longer I gazed, the more captivated I became. It was as
if I were being drawn into the eyes of a Vermeer—one that had
been turned inside out, and then folded back upon itself.

I blinked at the fascination stirring within. *What the hell am I thinking?* I shut my laptop and reached for the light.

She fluttered into my head during a board meeting the next day, and again the night after that. I thought of her tall frame and willowy arms. I imagined a cascade of hair as she kissed her way down my stomach. After an hour of tossing and turning, I reached for my laptop. Her picture gazed back.

Hello Zhanna. Quite interested in meeting you. I'm a professional woman, early thirties. Would like a discreet and understanding friend to spend time with. Look forward to hearing from you. G.

My finger hovered over the ENTER button for what seemed an eternity.

I checked messages while brushing my teeth, upon reaching the office, then at lunch. Nothing. Three o'clock found me chiding myself for being so foolish. For all I knew, some overweight, hairy guy might have placed the post wearing a stained T-shirt and socks, grinning as he chewed a mushy-ended cigar that had long gone out.

Just after four, a message popped up.

Hello G. Would be glad to meet. Let me know where and what time works best. Zhanna.

She sent along a picture, head slightly turned with a trace of a smile. It was date-stamped five minutes before. Her eyes appeared soft and kind. Genuine. I felt flushed all over. We agreed to meet Friday evening, at a quiet coffee shop in the next town.

Tracing a finger around the rim of my cup, I gazed out the window. People moved to and fro—doing errands, picking up pizza or just strolling. It didn't take much to gauge a couples' familiarity with one another. The middle-aged maintained a very slight distance between their shoulders, where younger pairs seemed inseparable—clutching one another around the waist as if letting go would be the death of them. An elderly man and his wife shuffled by. They were holding hands. It was hard for me to imagine spending that much time with one person—to need and be needed so much.

Perhaps my mother was right....

"You know, Glenda," she had said, "Maybe you should consider stepping away for a while."

"From my career? Why would I want to do that?"

"Take a little time for yourself. Enjoy the tapestry of life."

"Mom, you're aware that my so called 'tapestry' doesn't have a man woven into it, right?"

"Oh I know, sweetie, and that's fine. Doesn't matter either way, when you think about it. I just worry that you work too much. Might be time to let someone in. Be in a relationship, as it were."

"Not sure that the words *relationship* and *I* go together. Sounds a little like trying to mix vinegar and oil."

"Mmm," she had said. "Italian dressing is that way, but when you shake the bottle, it's delicious."

I blinked and pushed the memory aside. Still, as I watched the gray-haired couple moving farther from view, I couldn't help but smile.

A tall blonde caught my attention, hips rolling gently as she crossed the street. She wore a pink blouse and black low-rise jeans. Her legs seemed to go on forever. There was an air of self-confidence about her—the look of someone who is used to being looked at. And look they did. A few women, trying their best to be inconspicuous, turned their heads. A little wave drew her closer, and I introduced myself.

"Hello, Glenda," she said, Russian accent as warming as Svedka. Everything about her was very ladylike—the way she walked and sat, even the tossing back of her hair. My eyes wandered to take in a slight view of cleavage, and I reminded myself that this woman—tall, soft and very feminine—had something different beneath her panties. A heat flickered at the thought of slowly easing them down.

"I'm glad you not back out to meet," she said.

"You've been stood up before?"

"Ah, yes. Some women, perhaps, think they want someone different, then I suppose they get frightened."

Her marvelous pronunciation delivered the words differently. "Sum vemen, pelhaps, tink dey vant..." I swallowed against a sudden dryness. As we talked, I found myself lingering upon her face, enthralled by her light-gray eyes and the playing of her tongue.

"Truly? You are lawyer?" I nodded. "And so pretty! You fortunate to be smart, and pretty is like bonus, yes?"

I felt myself blushing, a smile pushing across my face. "Would you like some coffee or tea?"

"Tea, ah yes," she said. As her chair moved, I reached for her hand. When I touched her, miniature shock waves traveled up my arm and ricocheted along my spine. She looked, then brought a caressing thumb to the back of my hand. A slow breath left her slightly parted lips. Long lashes blinked, then opened to me.

"I have some at home," I whispered.

Tea in hand, we sat on the couch with legs curled beneath us. Norah Jones poured out her soul in the background. My ever-changing pulse was incapable of keeping time with the thump of the bass. I watched her tuck a length of hair behind an ear, reflection of the fireplace dancing in her eyes. I couldn't remember the last time I felt so many butterflies. It took a moment to register that her lips had moved.

"I'm sorry?"

She let out a giggle. "I say you look so much nervous. Are you all right?"

"Oh, yes, I—I'm sorry!"

She reached out and, after setting our cups aside, gently took my hands. A tingling spread through my arms. "I also nervous. A time for me since with a woman last. And you so very—so very beautiful, Glenda."

I edged closer. "Say my name again. Please."

She blinked and brought her lips beside me, hair faintly brushing upon my face. "Glenda," she whispered back— *Ghlendah* rolled within my ear.

Sliding my cheek along hers, I savored the softness of her lips. Our mouths mingled, pressed and yielded—tongues captured, circled and released. The fluttering within quickly became heat— smolder to flame. White chills moved from my lower back and nestled between my shoulders, leaving me to breathe in quick gasps. I took her hands and, slowly walking backward, kissed her all the way to the bedroom.

Fingers traced faces as we lay side by side. Her lips pressed urgently, softened and then grew hungry again. I welcomed and reached for them, pleading wordlessly. Back arching, I pressed as much of myself against her as I could, my toes curled. Noses moved from side to side as we nibbled and kissed—her gasps mirroring my own. One of her long legs slid atop mine and, as I yielded to the fire pulsing in my core, colors began to rise behind my eyelids. Hues of pink shifted to oranges and reds. I clenched. *Oh my god, I'm gonna come! Just kissing her is making me come!*

Easing Zhanna onto her back, I slipped atop. I took her wrists and, placing them over her head, watched as she lay there, waiting with lips slightly parted. I ran a solitary fingertip along her face and neck, tracing a slow line to her cleavage. Leaning in, I softly kissed her, undid the first button of her blouse and then moved back to see the newly exposed flesh. Kisses, a button, exposing another few inches—over and over, as if this were a slow, sultry dance. When I finished, her taut belly met my eyes. Her chin quaked as I skimmed my nails from the base of her neck to the top of her jeans.

Urging her upward, I slipped off her shirt and bra. My eyes drank in her small breasts—nipples hard as little pink candies. We fell together and I encircled her tits as we kissed, feeling the vibration of her moans. Her hands slid down my back, rounded my ass, then moved quickly to my shirt. As she undid the buttons, I slowly kissed my way downward.

Her back arched sharply as I took a nipple in my mouth, licking and sucking. She drew a long breath, held it, then let it out with a shudder. I shifted for her as she removed my shirt and bra. After loosening my pants, her fingers slipped beneath the fabric. She drew a slow line over the top edge of my panties, and then moved around and up my spine. I switched to her other breast. She cupped it, feeding it to me with one hand while her other moved along my side. She encircled one of my tits. Electricity surged as she gently kneaded, adding the random flicker of a fingernail.

My mouth left her breast. As I began a journey down her tense stomach, she pressed against my shoulders, urging me away. She slipped off the foot of the bed, and I wondered if I had gone too far—if I were being presumptuous as to what she desired. Zhanna eased the pants off my legs. Gathering up my clothes, she folded them neatly and set them on a side chair. She stood at the foot of the bed, a faint smile upon her lips. I watched as she undid her jeans and slowly stepped out of them, leaving each of us in panties. My eyes took in her long, smooth legs and the slight rounding of her hips. I could see the outline pressing against the underside of her lace.

As she crawled up the bed her long hair caressed my thighs and hips, stomach and breasts. When her blonde mane fell all around my face, seeming to shield us from the rest of the world, she kissed me softly. I cupped her cheeks. She took one of my hands and, laying my earlier fear to rest, brought it to the lump between her legs—moaning as I rubbed and squeezed.

With agonizing slowness, she kissed her way down my neck and set her mouth upon one of my nipples. Shock waves moved straight into my core as she nibbled and licked—one, the other, then back again. My hands, feeling as though they were no longer attached, ran softly over her face and arms, shoulders and breasts. The music of lovers filled my ears—the song of my panting interlacing seamlessly with her soft moans. My wetness pushed forth.

Her lips moved lower. With hair strewn all about, she kissed my navel, then one of my hips. Her tongue drew a slow line across the top of my panties as they began moving downward. As a ballerina might, I drew my legs out and opened myself to her.

Without any predictable rhythm or pattern, she tasted me. She kissed one part of my labia, flicked her tongue over my bud and then nibbled lightly on another spot of my sensitive, swollen lips. Her tongue moved hard up the length of my crease, paused to swirl my juices over my clit, then gently kissed her way all over me again. I was being consumed with deliberate slowness, like a delicacy.

I peered down at the scattering of hair. Taking her head in my hands, I urged her onto my aching clit and held her there. Her tongue assailed it, rubbing on and around me. I began to sear—back arching, hips shaking. Hands took my wrists and held them to my sides. She drew her mouth away.

"Please," I panted. "Please, don't stop!" She smiled, mouth wet and shimmering.

"Aah, I not stoppingh, Ghlendah," she whispered. Easing a pillow behind my head, she tossed her hair to one side, then moved back between my legs. "You cahn vatch me, if you vant. Vatch me as longh as you cahn."

With agonizing slowness, she began all over again. A lick, a kiss and a nibble—the sweet torment of her incredible mouth. My hands clutched the sheets as I watched her eyes flutter, blink softly, then close. She was not just eating me out, not just trying to get me off. She was making love to me. She tasted and took, gave and shared. Her mouth was my mouth—my flesh was her flesh. The kisses she was giving—those beautiful, eternal kisses—were the sort that brought poets to weep for not finding the words.

Time fell away as the pressure rose within. The sight of her there, the heat of her breath upon me—I was slipping out of myself as though there were no longer skin to contain me.

I grunted, groaned and cried out as my floodgates burst. Wave after wave crested and fell through me, spurned by her delight in tasting my juices. She stayed with me as I came, then came again—moving from one shuddering crescendo to another. Never had I trembled so much or rolled through so many explosions.

Zhanna kissed her way to my mouth and then, rolling onto her back, shared the taste of my nectar with me. I eased down her panties, her cock slipping between my breasts as I ventured down her stomach. Curving slightly, she was hard and wanting. I licked the sweet glistening from the tip, and then took her in.

She let out a long sigh, as my lips and tongue moved around and over her. The sensation of her, wet and hard and fitting so well within my mouth, sent sparks down my spine once again. Her head fell back in ecstasy, framed by the rise of her cute breasts. I bobbed and swirled and worked her hot tool, sighs and moans filling my ears. I went as far as I could, then sucked hard all the way back to the tip.

I tongued the underside of her length, to where her hairless balls awaited. Very gently, I licked and sucked one, then the other. Her knees came up and I could feel her thighs quivering. Lips pulling one ball harder, I was rewarded with a sigh, then gave the other the same hungry attention.

Taking her shaft back in my mouth, I moved one of my hands to my saturated pussy. My finger moved, slowly at first, then with more urgency. A second finger followed. Thoroughly coated, I brought them to rest against her tightly puckered hole. She opened like a butterfly, and I slowly pressed in.

Moans filled my ears. One of her hands lightly cupped my cheek, the other moved beneath to take my wrist. She eased my fingers deeper, hips riding both my hand and mouth. Staggered breaths escaped her, and I felt a white heat flaring up in my core. Her ass tightened, wand dancing within my mouth.

After a collection of moments, her fingers cupped my face, urging me off. Her chin quivered as I let my fingers travel a few more times before slowly easing out.

She laid me on my back and raised my hips until I was nearly resting on my shoulders. Squatting over me, she reached behind and pulled her sack out of view, holding it against her butt. She slipped into me—my pussy clenching her, welcoming her. Watching that beautiful shaft sliding between us, it became difficult to tell who it belonged to.

The glistening rod found my spot. A rainbow flashed behind my eyelids and I began to shudder. With her hair swaying all around, I cupped her breasts, thumbs moving rapidly over nipples. My earthquake intensified, moans echoing back.

I held her tight as she lowered me, keeping her within my

clutching walls. Lips and tongues mingled, becoming more urgent as we rocked and ground against each other. Our hands were everywhere—rounding breasts, moving through hair and traveling down necks. Her hard nipples pressed against my own.

Our eruptions rose, burst forth and overtook us—hot waves pulsating and pushing in unison. Gasping, sweating, shaking, I felt my world teeter, then fall away...so very far away.

Soft kisses found lips and cheeks, earlobes and necks. We soon became still and quiet, arms and legs intertwined. My core eased to embers.

Deep within, something shifted and gave way, like a mountain shedding a precarious, snowy overhang. I swallowed against the hardness in my throat, then, unable to fight it any longer, yielded with a sigh. A tear crested and began to journey. She drew it in with a kiss. Moments became minutes uncounted, settling atop one another like feathers from a torn pillow.

Eventually she stirred, the tip of her nose moving lightly upon my cheek. "Pelhaps I should goh," floated her whisper.

"Will you stay with me, Zhanna?" I traced the edge of her face. "Will you stay until morning?"

CHATTEL

Errica Liekos

Shortly after they got married, Alex had told Sasha, "Do what you want. I love you, and I don't ever want to stop you from being you. If you want to be with me, be with me. If not, don't. I won't stop you. I want you to be happy."

Her friends thought it was romantic. A man who wasn't jealous, who didn't get weird about girls' night out, or get mad when she wanted to go to book club or knitting circle instead of serving him a beer while he watched the game. She could just do whatever she wanted, when she wanted; total freedom. They acted like it was a dream come true.

Sasha wasn't so sure.

For her birthday last year, he'd gotten her coupons for a couple's massage...for her and a friend. She took Lucy. The year before, it had been tickets to the ballet, with a suggestion that she take Regina. He hated the ballet, so she did. He knew she didn't enjoy softball and didn't ask her to come with him when he played. Once they even went to a movie theater and split up to watch different movies when they couldn't agree on documentary (him) or action (her). She did all the things she would have gotten to do if she was still single.

Sasha was miserable and hadn't a clue what she was supposed to complain about. She tried talking to some of her friends about it and ended up getting lectures on women's rights and the history of marriage.

"Women used to be chattel," Lucy scolded, "and you're telling me you want your husband to be *more* possessive of you? What next, you're going to take his last name?"

"Fine, you can trade husbands with me," Regina said. "I'll take the man who wants us to see *Swan Lake* and you can have the man who tells me I put the 'bitch' in 'Stitch-and-Bitch' every single time I leave the house for knitting circle. You don't know how good you've got it, honey."

Sasha didn't want to give up her maiden name, and she didn't want Alex to turn passive-aggressive on her, but yes, she thought, she did want him to be more possessive. Maybe he *should* demand that she show up to root for him at his softball games, and maybe he should make her watch the movie he wanted, just because he wanted it, and wanted her company at the same time.

So when she opened her latest birthday present over dinner at a Turkish restaurant to find a pair of opera tickets, she couldn't keep quiet any longer.

"I don't want to keep going to these things alone."

"What do you mean?" Alex said. "There're two tickets."

"But you don't want to go with me."

"So you should miss out on *Don Giovanni* because I don't like it? Come on, who's that girlfriend of yours who's into opera, too? Lucy? Jessie?"

"It's Lucy," said Sasha. "Jesse is a guy. You want me to take another man to the opera with me?"

"If that's who you want to take, I'm not going to stop you."

Sasha slammed her hands down into her lap in frustration, knocking her napkin to the floor. "I want to take *you*. But I know you don't like opera, which means my choices for enjoying *your* birthday present to me are to make you miserable or be without you. Doesn't that seem a little wrong to you?"

Alex leaned forward, crossing his arms on the table. "Okay. Tell me what's going on."

"It's just that...marriage is compromise, right?"

"It doesn't have to be."

"Yes, Alex, I think it does. I can't do all the things I did when I was single and still be the kind of wife I want to be. Or have you be the husband I want you to be." Sasha trailed off. Alex's expression was unreadable.

"Go on."

"You're so focused on us each doing our own thing." Her voice dropped to almost a whisper. "Sometimes I feel like you don't really want to be married to me."

Sasha didn't order her usual dessert, and Alex skipped his coffee. They drove home in silence. Sasha felt like crying. Regina was right; she had the perfect man, and she didn't appreciate him. He'd dressed in his best suit, given her a chance to wear a new dress, taken her to a lovely dinner, and bought her a present that showed he thought of what she liked at the expense of his own preferences. And now he was pissed off at her, and she'd ruined everything.

Alex used his key to open the door to their apartment, then stepped aside to let Sasha enter first. She stepped into the dark, intending to turn on the hallway light, but Alex closed the front door before she could reach it. She felt his hand close around the back of her neck, stopping her forward movement. She stumbled, and his other arm wrapped around her waist and caught her. She felt his hot breath as he began to speak, close and low, into her ear.

"Maybe I haven't been making myself clear," Alex said. "I let you go because I trust you to come back. Men like me don't give away things they're unsure of. But maybe you haven't understood my confidence in you."

"I..." Sasha started to speak, but Alex's hand tightened behind her neck, and she stopped. He rubbed his five o'clock shadow against her throat, then continued.

"I can see now that I made a mistake," he said. "You don't need your freedom, do you? You need to know you're wanted. You need to know you're loved."

Sasha felt her legs go weak. She leaned on Alex, and he held her weight. There were no windows in their front hall. She opened and closed her eyes to the same solid black.

"I'll be clear from here on out. You're mine. I own you. I tell you to spend time with your friends because it gives me pleasure to do so. Because I like you missing me, and I like it when you come home with new stories from your friends and your world to entertain me. I expect you to stay independent and entertaining to me. Do you understand?"

Sasha nodded.

"Because I have no interest in owning something weak and unchallenging, Sasha. I want you strong, and I want you to have your own interests." Alex lowered his voice even more. "But you belong to me. Do you understand?"

Sasha nodded again.

"I'm not sure you do. Go into the living room. I'm going to show you."

Alex released her, and she walked deeper into their apartment, less sure in her heels than she'd ever felt before, sensing his body just a few inches behind her with every step. She turned the corner, and their living room appeared before her, lit by the streetlamps shining through the windows. She hesitated at the doorway.

"The middle of the room will be fine."

Sasha moved to the center of the room, and hesitated again.

"Face me."

She did. Alex had his arms crossed, but his body language didn't seem closed off. There was a trace of a smile dancing around his lips.

"It really is a lovely dress you're wearing," he said. "Take it off."

Sasha blinked, then did as she was told. A pile of green silk quickly landed in a puddle around her feet.

"And matching underwear, too. Lovely." Alex stepped forward and ran a hand along her side, like he was calming a skittish horse. "But I want you, not some fancy outfit. Take them off as well, if you please."

The courtesy of his phrasing somehow made the words even less of a request, more of a command. She unhooked her bra and let it fall. She slid down her panties and stepped out of them, then nudged the clothing away from herself with one foot, so she wouldn't trip on the fabric. Sasha looked down at her high heels and back up at Alex.

"Shoes, too?"

He chuckled. "Let's not go nuts."

Sasha stood in front of her husband, naked except for three-inch black leather heels. He was close enough to touch, close enough that she could grasp him with both arms and cling to him for reassurance, but she didn't dare. She held still as he watched her, his eyes roaming over her body, finally meeting her eyes.

"Good girl," he said.

She shivered.

"Oh," Alex said. "I see. Let's warm you up." He knelt down in front of her, reached for her hip and kissed her.

Sasha had never really liked anyone, even Alex, going down on her. It made her self-conscious. Without thinking, she stepped back.

Alex stood up faster than she realized was possible, grabbed her upper arm and yanked her body back toward his own.

"See?" he said, pressing against her. "This is what I'm talking about. I'm not doing this for *you*. This is what *I* want." He took her other arm in his hand as well and started walking forward, forcing her to walk back. Each time she took a misstep in her heels, his arms supported her. "You belong to me. All of you. I don't care if this makes you nervous, I don't care if you don't understand how beautiful and delicious I find you." Sasha took a final step backward and felt the fabric of their couch against the backs of her legs. "Now lie down, spread your legs and give it over."

Sasha felt the heat and moisture building between her legs. She did as instructed.

"Better," Alex said. He knelt again between her legs, lifting one up onto the back of the couch, knocking the other so her calf hung over the edge and her shoe rested on the floor. She felt his breath and then his tongue on her lips and clit, and she moaned.

"Behave yourself or I'll tie you down," he murmured, and went back to work, alternately licking, nibbling and sucking on the sensitive flesh. She tried to stay quiet for him, but soon enough was moaning in a different way. Her self-consciousness was gone. He wasn't doing it because he thought he had to. He wasn't trying to impress her; he was trying to devour her. His tongue slid all the way inside her, then out again to investigate her folds. She had no obligations other than to be his toy, and this knowledge changed the entire experience for her. She felt the couch getting wetter and wetter beneath her and knew that it wasn't his saliva that was the culprit. She moaned again and started thrusting her hips into his mouth. When her legs started to quiver, he stopped.

"Not yet," he said. He stood and backed up a few steps. "Kneel."

Sasha pulled herself off the couch and sank to the carpet in front of him. Her head was level with the bulge in his pants.

"Take it out."

Sasha unfastened his belt, unzipped his fly and lowered his pants just enough to release his cock.

"Suck me," he said. "No hands."

Sasha gently closed her mouth over the head of his cock and began working up and down the shaft.

"Suck harder," he said. "Not faster, just harder. That's it. Let it almost come out of your mouth, then take as much as you can."

Sasha tried to oblige, but after only a few strokes, she let him slide out of her mouth altogether. She reached up to put him back, and Alex caught her wrists.

"That's too bad," he said. He sounded amused. "I said no hands." Sasha opened her mouth, but he cut her off before she could get a word out. "I believe I also said that if you didn't behave, I'd tie you down."

Still holding her wrists in one hand, he stripped his belt out of the loops on his pants with the other. He bent down and placed the belt against her lips.

"Hold this."

Sasha looked into her husband's eyes. What she saw made

her open her mouth, then close it obediently over the leather.

"Good girl," he said again, and she knelt up straighter for him. He put her hands behind her back, then held out his free hand for the belt again. She bent her head down and dropped it into his palm. He leaned over her and tied her hands behind her back with the belt, sliding it through the buckle until it was tight on her wrists, then looping the excess leather through the center and closing her hands over her own restraint to hold it in place. The tail of the leather hung down along the crack of her ass and on her ankles before coming to rest on the floor.

"Very nice." Alex tilted his head near hers and smiled gently. "Your nipples tightened up again. It's so obvious that you like this, I can't imagine why I didn't do it before." He straightened up, and his cock was in her face again. "Try again."

Sasha did. She sucked with the strength and speed Alex demanded, and she bobbed her head to chase after his cock, regaining her suction as quickly as possible each time after he slid from her mouth. She felt the roof of her mouth pressing down tight on him, and reveled in the noises her throat made as it grasped and released him. Alex reached for the back of her neck, slid his hand up into her hair, then closed his fist on a huge handful of her mane. Sliding out was no longer a risk as he pumped her head up and down his shaft, steady, strong and fast, until he moaned himself and came, holding her tight and still with his cock deep in her mouth, shooting down her throat as she struggled to swallow and suck and breathe all at once. Slowly his grip on her hair lessened, and she withdrew.

"That," Alex said, "was perfect." He tucked himself back into his clothing, refastened his pants, then hooked his hands under her arms and stood her up. Then he spun her around and released her wrists from his belt. "But we're not done. I believe," he continued, as she turned back to him, "that you were interrupted earlier." He gave her a little push, and she landed on the couch with a bounce. "It's your birthday, so I'm going to make it easy for you." He pressed her shoulders down onto the cushions and spread her wide apart. Then he took her hand and placed it between her legs.

"Show me," he said. He undid his tie and wrapped it over her eyes, plunging her into blackness again. "Let me know when you get close."

She couldn't remember ever being so wet before. Her finger circled her clit, and it barely qualified as friction. She began using her whole hand, and soon the feel of Alex's fingers on her nipples and his breath on her thigh pushed her over the edge.

Sasha gasped. "Now," she said. "Now."

Alex bent to her clit and drew her into his mouth. His tongue was her world as she came.

The next day, Alex came home with another package wrapped in birthday-patterned foil. Sasha opened it and found a thin, soft, black leather collar with a small ring in the front. Her eyes widened.

"Where did you get this?"

"Never mind," Alex said. "I got it, and that's enough." He took the collar out of her hands and showed her the metal loop built into the buckle. Then he pulled her into the bathroom and in front of the sink so she faced the mirror. He stood behind her, and she watched while he fastened the collar around her neck.

"The buckle can be locked," he said, "but for now I'll trust you to wear it when I tell you to. You'll take Lucy to the opera this Saturday, not Jesse. And you'll wear this all evening until you get home. You can put it on yourself, but I'm the only one allowed to take it off. And next time, you're going to need to ask permission to come. Do you understand?"

Sasha nodded. She felt the heat growing between her legs

again as she leaned back against her husband and raised one hand to stroke the leather and hook a finger into the collar's ring. She smiled, wondering if Alex had already bought a leash to clip on to her collar, and wondering how exactly she was going to conceal the collar from—or explain it to—her friend Lucy.

REVEALING

Ruby Ryder

Placing another piece of steak in her mouth, Cindy made adorable *yummy* noises that make Jack laugh. Okay, so he could definitely cook. After three months of dating, he'd finally insisted she come to his house so he could cook dinner for her. She'd been resisting going to his place and wasn't even sure why. He seemed eager to show off his skills in the kitchen, though, so she finally said yes. Why not check out his ability to cook and keep house? Jack's skills in bed had already been tested during their encounters at her apartment. Cindy smiled a little thinking about that.

He was a sweet, handsome, intelligent guy…but Cindy wasn't yet convinced they were a good match. She'd been looking for signs that Jack was…adventuresome…in bed. No luck yet. He was talented, knew what to do with his fingers, tongue and lovely cock…but so far had shown no signs of kink. She was still hoping.

Their relationship was new. Perhaps he didn't feel comfortable revealing too much too soon. She laughed inwardly—she was doing the same thing, right? She didn't want to reveal her predilection for rather unusual fetishes until she got some indication they might be well received. Wouldn't it be funny if they were both doing the same thing? It would. But the risk lay in making the first move...revealing first. Who would be the one to take the chance? Then there was always the possibility there was nothing to reveal on his end. That was the chance she took dating a vanilla guy. But even the vanilla guys could rally when given the opportunity. Even vanilla guys dreamed of kinky sex.

She eyed the rib-eye steak, rice pilaf and oven-roasted asparagus on her plate. Every bite was well worth a yummy noise. She took a drink of the expensive champagne. Jack had impressed her. With the food, certainly, but he had a nice place, too. Not what she had expected, not the usual single guy living by himself type of feel. Clean, comfortable, with actual decorative touches here and there. She liked it here. She liked Jack. So she really hoped he would turn out to be at least a little kinky.

"Oh my god this is incredible! Where did you learn to cook like this?" she mumbled through her bite of steak.

"My mom." He smiled. "I was always in the kitchen with her... probably because I like to eat so much." They both laughed.

They'd met in an unlikely place. At the top of Nordhoff Peak. Cindy had been in the mood for a long hike and couldn't find anyone to join her, so she decided to go by herself. What an interesting hike it turned out to be.

Sometimes she preferred solo hiking because of the mental space and freedom it offered. The seven-mile hike to the peak was strenuous but doable. Cindy was resting at the top, drinking in the view and enjoying the endorphin rush. She pulled out her lunch and had just started eating when up walked Jack...hiking alone as well. Apparently he had started a half an hour later than she had, even parked at the same trailhead. They ate lunch and then hiked back together, talking the whole way. After that, dating each other felt rather predestined.

Cindy considered what she knew about Jack so far: he owned a landscaping company with several employees. He was used to doing hard work. Medium in height and stocky in build, Jack had large hands that could be remarkably gentle and talented at lovemaking. Intense blue eyes contrasted with his tanned face in a way that captivated her. His blond hair was kept in a longish cut, just enough for her to run her fingers through. Jack loved to be in the mountains and could be found hiking the hills on his off days. They'd enjoyed a couple more hikes since they met. He could actually keep up with her! Many men couldn't. All that was good. But he seemed so...normal. Not that normal was bad...just not what she preferred when it came to sex.

Cindy worked as a waitress in a very expensive gourmet restaurant. Her coworkers were often amazed that such a tiny woman could actually carry those large trays filled with plates of food, but Cindy was no slacker. She lifted weights and worked out at the gym regularly. Though small, she was quite strong. She could dress it up when necessary but was a tomboy at heart, a woman who would rather be out hiking than at a fancy dinner. Dark brown hair fell to her waist and was usually tied back in a braid. With soft brown eyes and a natural beauty that didn't need makeup, she got her share of attention.

Her appearance was deceptive. She tended to attract men who were looking for a woman who was rather wholesome... nothing resembling the wanton wench that inhabited her small frame. She could throw a good fuck and was proud of it. She could make men whimper and tremble and swoon. Not all of them wanted to...she'd found. That was the tricky part. She had to find out what side of the fence Jack stood on.

So what was she waiting for? Time to 'fess up to the kink! Still, she hesitated. They finished dinner, the conversation interesting but unremarkable...what she really wanted to be talking about was sex. Kinky sex, specifically. She could feel it coming... the moment when she'd lay her cards out on the table and hope for the best.

She helped him clear the table and automatically opened the dishwasher to load it with the dinner dishes. She pulled out the top shelf and her eyes went straight to it.

Well Holy Fuck, Batman! *Jackpot.*

"Oh! We don't have to do these dishes tonight...let's just leave them." His hand stopped the shelf from coming all the way out, pushing it back in with too much insistence and closing the dishwasher door. Jack pressed her against the kitchen counter, kissing her deeply. Jack could make her wet with his kisses, so she let him have his way for a while.

When they came up for air she murmured, "Too late, Jack...I saw it." Watching his face carefully for reaction, she saw surprise, embarrassment and uncertainty.

"Really...well. Okay then." He laughed nervously.

"Hey, babe—toys are cool. Totally." Cindy turned around, opened up the dishwasher, slid out the top shelf and grabbed the large black dildo. "This is actually pretty impressive, Jack."

Jack was blushing crimson, despite his tan skin. He looked uncomfortable, even after her obvious approval of the toy.

"But it's not as big as mine..." She grinned at him.

"Yours...uhhhh...what?" Something wasn't computing in his head. And then she watched it click in.

"Where's the harness? I want to see it," she said lightly.

"Harness? Ummm, actually...I don't have one."

Okay. Jack was sort of coming apart at the seams, Cindy could tell, poor guy. It was as if he didn't want to admit what he used the dildo for, wasn't sure if they were on the same page or not and was still scared to...reveal. But come on, what else would he be using a dildo for?

Cindy pulled him by his neck down to her lips and kissed him passionately.

"Jack..." She held the dildo up between them and ran her fingers down the length of it. "This is for...your ass...right?"

Jack looked down and just nodded, unable to get any words out. She lifted his eyes back to hers with a touch under his chin.

"I think that is so....fucking...hot." There. He couldn't mistake that.

"...Seriously?" Jack looked doubtful, but his cock was hard against her, entertaining no such doubts.

"Way seriously." Cindy disengaged from his embrace and placed the dildo in his hands.

"Hang on to that.... I'll be right back." She walked out of the kitchen toward the front door.

"But...where are you—?" Jack sputtered.

"Don't worry, Jack. I am so coming back." She scampered happily out to her car and snatched her toy bag from the back-seat. On a whim she'd thrown it in, hoping for the courage to tell Jack that she was a kinky bitch after which she hoped he'd enthusiastically just go with the program. She'd never been so happy that she'd followed a whim.

Literally skipping back to the door, she came in to find Jack exactly where she'd left him in the kitchen. He still looked a tad bewildered. She took his hand and led him to the couch, sitting down and patting the couch next to her as she opened the red velvet bag. Jack sat down, still holding the dildo in one hand and looking like he wasn't sure what to do with it. This felt inevitable, Cindy thought, but there was always a possibility things could go wrong, even at this point. So she chose her words cautiously.

"Jack, listen carefully. It's all good, honey. I love that you're into ass play. Guess what? So am I! Look, I'll show you." Jack's eyes got big when she pulled out a purple dildo and took the black one from him, putting them side by side. "See? I told you yours was bigger!" She laughed. Jack joined in, finally starting to relax a little.

"No fucking way, Cindy! You gotta be kidding me!" His eyes sparkled and he couldn't have been smiling any bigger.

"Oh, but wait...there's more!" She glanced back and forth and lowered her voice conspiratorially. "Not only do you get the dildo and the steak knives..." She giggled. "You get the handy-dandy, ultra-sexy...dildo holder!"

Cindy pulled out her supple black harness and the scent of luxurious leather came with it. Her antics inspired raucous laughter from them both.

"We have the technology!" Her words spurred even more frivolity. Cindy took the black dildo and put it through the O-ring, snapping the tabs back into place. She held it up for Jack to see. The bulge in his jeans spoke volumes. His eyes were filled with a deep and immediate need as he looked at her. She stood up, grabbed Jack's hand and pulled him into the bedroom.

"I am so going to slide this right up your ass and fuck you. Get those clothes off, right now." She could tell that Jack could barely contain himself.

"I like it when you use that tone, Cindy." Jack's voice was rough. He was naked and standing before her in record time, stroking his stiff cock. Cindy tried to race him, but he was so fast she didn't stand a chance. When she was finally as naked as he was, his words registered and she looked up quickly.

"Seriously?" She eyed him intently.

"Cindy, I have never been more serious in my life." Jack's face was open and filled with such a longing it shook her a little. He knelt before her diminutive frame.

"I...am yours."

Three words, so powerful in their meaning and stark simplicity. She felt the wetness and throbbing of desire between her legs. This was a fucking dream come true. And to think she was afraid he wouldn't be kinky. Not only was Jack kinky, he was precisely the right kind of kinky. What were the chances?

"Oh, Jack." She motioned for him to stand up and they kissed. She pulled him hard against her. One hand snaked between them and she squeezed his cock, caressed his balls. He was standing at the foot of the bed, and she pushed him backward onto it with no warning. His arms flailed at first and then he laughed and relaxed into his fall.

Cindy climbed on top of him and sat her juicy wetness right down on his firm cock. She closed her eyes and began to slide back and forth slowly, pushing his hard cock against his belly to thrill her clit, riding the ridge of it.

"No coming until I give you permission, Jack." Her words had an edge and she felt his cock throb in response before he answered. Excellent.

"Yes, Ma'am."

Oh baby! *Jackpot with Jack.* Silly things like that ran through her head until the sensation of her wet, slick cunt on his rock-hard cock took over everything. Heaven. Cindy rode him just like that, angling her body for the most intensity. His cock was hers to enjoy. He was hers.

"May I?" His words were spoken softly, as if hesitant to

interrupt. Cindy opened her eyes and saw Jack's hands poised in front of her breasts.

"Yes." The word was breathy with her excitement. Jack knew what she liked. He flicked her nipples and lightly pinched them, sending currents of electricity straight to her pussy. She sped up her motion and pressed her clit harder against Jack's raging cock. She was almost there.

This man was hers! The thought of his submission, and fiery scenes of what she intended to do with that gift, pushed her over the edge into a sweet, pulsing orgasm with waves of quivering bliss. She stopped sliding and lay down against him, kissing him deeply. Jack ran his hands up and down her back, meeting her dancing tongue with soft lips. His cock was soaked, and he'd never even been inside her.

"Well done, Jack." He smiled at her postorgasmic half-lidded sensuality. Cindy rolled off him slowly and padded out to her toy bag, still on the couch. She grabbed some lube and brought it into the bedroom, throwing it on the bed. Then she stepped into her harness, the big black dildo waving in front of her, and buckled it firmly in place. Jack watched with lust in his eyes.

"Time for the tell-all, Jack. Have you ever been fucked?"

"No, Ma'am."

"Have you had this baby completely in your ass before?" She grabbed the dildo as she spoke.

"Yes, Ma'am. Many times." Cindy smiled. The word jackpot came in her mind for the third time that night. Okay, time for a new metaphor. This was so much better than any jackpot she'd ever won at Vegas! Jack was like a gift that just kept on giving.

"How much warm-up do you need?"

"Well...none, Ma'am."

"Jack...I am impressed!" He smiled, just a little embarrassed.

She climbed on the bed and gestured for him to move over, lying down where he'd just been.

"Ride it, baby." She pointed to her cock as she slathered it with lube.

Jack straddled her and took the bottle of lube from her. He squirted some on his fingers, reached back and applied it to his ass. Cindy watched with fascination. His eyes were closed and his hips were undulating a bit as he worked his fingers in a little. Then Jack positioned himself over Cindy, placing the head of her dildo against his ass.

"May I?" He didn't need her permission, but seemed to want to ask for it anyway.

"You may." She nodded.

Jack slowly sank down onto her toy, moving his hips slightly to help get the head in. His mouth opened with pleasure and he moaned. He let himself down gradually until he sat lightly on her, the entire dildo inside his ass. Cindy gave him a little time to adjust.

She did not often play the part of the pillow princess with a strap-on. Normally she was all about thrusting and driving her toy deep into her partner's ass. But tonight she was in the mood to watch Jack...fuck himself. And what a show it looked like it was going to be. His blond hair messy and curly, strands of it fell on his forehead. His muscular chest and farmer's tan were magnificent, and those thighs were surely strong enough to keep him going for a long time. They'd better be.

"Okay, Jack, I want to see fifty long, slow strokes. Count them aloud. And don't you dare come." Cindy smiled wickedly.

"As you wish, Ma'am." Jack's brows were drawn together in that look of painful passion as he began to ride...and count. He whimpered and gasped and moaned between his counting.

Once she thrust off the bed deep into him with no warning and got an "Oh!"

He managed to get to fifty and his cock was leaking a steady stream of precome onto her belly. She slicked her fingers in it and rubbed the head of his cock, making him gasp. She stroked his cock a few times, spreading the puddle on her belly all over his cock.

"Oh! God! Cindy... Ahhh!"

Jack was trying so hard not to come. She was purposely pushing that line, stroking his cock, enjoying the desperate tone in his voice. Normally, desperation did not please her. But a situation where the desperation involved a man trying so very hard not to cross over the line into ecstasy? She loved that dynamic. She loved the control. And Jack was turning out to be very... controllable.

"Another fifty." Her voice was stern and she looked him right in the eye when she said it.

He hesitated just a moment. "...If it pleases you, Ma'am." He said the words right back at her, never looking away. He was breathing hard and his thighs were trembling...but he began again.

This time it was so evident that he was right on the edge that she didn't dare touch his cock. The stream of liquid from his cock increased, as did his moans.

He'd reached thirty-five when Cindy ordered, "Stop." His relief was obvious.

"Listen carefully, Jack...I want you to complete the last fifteen without stopping for any reason. Got it?"

"Yes I do, Ma'am."

Cindy grabbed his cock and said, "And I'd do them quickly if I were you...."

She began pumping Jack's cock and she watched him

suddenly understand her intent. He started bouncing hurriedly on her cock and immediately felt his orgasm build past the point of holding it back as her hand matched his rhythm.

"Four, five, six, seven!" Jack managed to get in two more strokes down onto Cindy's toy before his come started shooting all over Cindy's breasts. Now each stroke in his ass and on his cock was almost unbearable with extra-sensitive sensations.

"AHH! Ten, eleven, TWELVE!!" He yelled the numbers. She knew what a mix of pain/pleasure this was...how much he wanted to stop...but he kept going! She took pity on Jack and stroked only his shaft.

"Thirteen! Fourteen Oh GOD!" He let out a sob and lifted himself one more time and slid back down. "Fifteen!" She pumped his cock, which was starting to soften, one last stroke. Then she let it go and watched him tremble for a while with complete sensory overload. She beckoned him down to her. Her cock still planted in his ass, Jack leaned heavily into her arms, still making small sounds in the back of his throat with each breath.

Cindy kissed him tenderly and stroked his back and neck as he calmed down. Eventually he climbed off that big black dildo and collapsed next to her, speechless. Cindy took off the harness and took it to the bathroom, leaving it in the sink and returning with a warm wet towel she used to clean them both up. Jack could hardly stand the touch of the towel on his cock, it was so sensitive. Cindy took Jack into her arms and held him, his face on her chest. His breathing slowly returned to normal.

She pulled the covers up and turned out the light as Jack faded off to sleep.

He...is mine.

NYOTAIMORI

Rose de Fer

I am lying as I have been trained. On my back, perfectly still. My knees are bent, my legs open and rotated out to the sides by 180 degrees. My feet are pressed together, sole to sole. Red silk ropes bind my ankles and wind gracefully around my knees to where they are fastened underneath the table, keeping me open, exposed. My arms are crossed in the small of my back and bound beneath me. The position forces my back to arch, pushing my chest up and out. I feel like a butterfly, pinned and displayed for a discriminating collector. A connoisseur.

They have given us all Japanese flower names and I am secretly pleased with mine: *Oniyuri*. It's the word for tiger lily, my favorite flower. They said it matched my flame-colored hair, my simmering passion.

The table beneath me is warm, but the food presented on my naked skin is not. A rainbow of sashimi is fanned across my belly: salmon, tuna, mackerel and yellowtail. Across my ribs is an array of sushi. Between my breasts are cuts of eel, drizzled with rich teriyaki sauce. And carefully arranged around my nipples are clutches of salmon roe, the eggs vibrant and bursting. Soft purple orchids frame my sex, and in the diamond formed by my spread and angled legs is a painted flask of warm sake.

I breathe slowly, shallowly, so as not to disturb the presentation of food. The smell is intoxicating and I long for a bite of fish, the tingle of ginger and wasabi on my tongue. But for now I am merely a decoration, an attractive display for the artfully arranged delicacies. In other rooms, other girls are bound as I am, their bodies serving the same erotic aesthetic. From somewhere I can hear the melancholy notes of a *shamisen* being played by one of the hostesses.

I feel the cool touch of Ayame's fingers as she gently lifts the flask from between my legs. My body heat has warmed the sweet wine and I close my eyes, listening to the soft splash as she fills each guest's cup. The sleeve of her silk kimono brushes my skin as she moves past me. When she is done she replaces the flask, pressing it firmly up against my sex. I imagine her playful smile as I resist the temptation to squirm against it.

"*Kanpai!*" say the two couples seated around me. They drink deeply after the toast and I listen for the clatter of chopsticks as their eyes roam over the food on offer.

My senses are highly attuned to the slightest sound, the slightest scent. The lady to my right is wearing a beautiful fragrance that has something of jasmine in it. It mingles with the salty fish, creating a strange perfume of its own. I think of serene Japanese gardens and koi ponds.

She is the first to select a bite. I lie motionless as her chopsticks skillfully lift a slice of fish from my belly and she sighs with pleasure at its taste. My chest barely rises as I breathe.

"Delicious," she says, her voice low and husky.

The man across from her at my left shoulder must be her

husband. He goes next, choosing one of the sushi rolls farther up my body. He prods my ribs with his chopsticks, deliberately I suspect. But I am too well trained to react. There is as much an art to eating from a woman's body as from being the platter that presents the food. My mouth waters and my sex moistens but those are the only responses I am allowed.

The pair sitting on either side of my lower half discusses where to begin. They have soft American accents and I add blue California skies to the images in my head. They choose together, symmetrically, snatching up two pieces of dragon roll from opposite sides and exclaiming over the taste.

Ayame refills their sake cups, this time grinding the flask a little harder against me as she replaces it. I smile inwardly at her challenge, enjoying the tingle it sends up through my body. I already have gooseflesh from the cold food arrayed on my skin and my nipples have puckered beneath the salmon roe.

One by one the sashimi slices and maki rolls and nigiri rolls disappear from my flesh. The American lady comments that it's like uncovering a hidden treasure.

The jasmine lady's husband chuckles at that. "And such a treasure," he says. He gently removes a single salmon egg the size of a pea from the clutch with his chopsticks and lifts it to my mouth. I imagine he is keen to make me react in some inappropriate manner. Perhaps he wants to see me punished. My pulse quickens at the thought.

My eyes convey nothing but gratitude for his offering as he places the tiny soft egg against my lips. With only the slightest movement I part them just enough to taste the salty juice with the tip of my tongue. It is heavenly. I close my eyes as I slowly draw the egg inside my mouth, bursting it between my teeth. It's only one little taste, one tiny bit of flavor, but it makes me sigh with pleasure. It mingles with the delicious scents all around me.

The fish, the ginger, wasabi and soy sauce, his wife's perfume...
I feel myself growing even damper against the flask of sake, and
I clench my inner muscles to intensify the sensation.

I hear Ayame's soft laugh. I might conceal my secret maneuvers from the guests, but I can never hide anything from her. My
eyes meet hers and she smiles. Her face is slightly flushed, and I
imagine I can smell her own desire beneath the silken kimono.

"Drink with us," the American man says.

He holds out his sake cup but Ayame shakes her head
demurely and produces one of her own, murmuring her gratitude as she sits at the end of the table. I can't help imagining how
much more exposed I would feel with my feet separated, my legs
splayed and tied together beneath the table, my dampening sex
on shameless display.

Looking down the length of my body I can just make out the
top of her head, her glossy black hair swept into an elaborate
geisha style. She is the only Japanese girl in the restaurant, a fact
that lends her both mystery and playful authority. She allows her
fingers to brush against my nether lips as she takes the flask to fill
her cup. This time she doesn't put it back. This time she leaves me
wholly on display and my heart starts to beat a little faster.

The jasmine lady scoops up some salmon roe with her chopsticks and her husband immediately does the same. Slowly,
slowly they pluck the eggs from me, a few at a time, until they
are almost gone. My breasts are smeared with the oily residue
and my nipples tighten even more as their movements send cool
air over the dampness. I suppress a little shiver.

Only a few pieces of fish and rice remain. If the guests want
more the chef will oblige, bringing it out on a wooden platter
and carefully placing each specially crafted piece on my body,
arranging everything as before. Then the process will begin
again. I hope they're still hungry.

But the American couple seems satisfied. They dab their lips with their napkins and express their appreciation for the food—and its display. I feel their cool fingers on my skin as they stroke me like a pet.

"What a good girl," the American lady says.

Her husband corrects her. "Good little dish."

They laugh softly.

Her long red nails travel over my belly to my pelvis, then down my inner thighs. A slight gasp escapes my throat, but I remain absolutely still. Only my skin betrays the excitement of her touch.

"Sayonara," she whispers. "Until next time." Then they slip away, padding silently out of the room.

Lady Jasmine and her husband aren't ready to leave yet and I'm filled with excitement. I sense they want more than just the decadent meal. The man gently gathers the last of the salmon roe from my left breast and holds it up. For a moment I think he's going to offer it to me. Then he asks Ayame if she'd like a bite.

She smiles. "Yes, please."

There is the rustle of silk as she leans forward to accept his offering. A soft, warm weight rests against my belly and I have to work to maintain my calm breathing. Her kimono is not at all traditional, and it is tied very loosely. A glance down shows me her beautiful pale breasts resting against my skin. They glisten with oil when she resumes her seat.

Lady Jasmine carefully plucks the last eggs from my right side, collecting them one by one and eating them with little sighs of pleasure. Each time her chopsticks come teasingly close to my nipples I hold my breath, longing to feel the touch of the cool, lacquered wood. But she manages to avoid even brushing me. Her control is maddening. My breasts are bare now. Only a thin sheen of salmon oil remains.

"Shall we start again?" her husband asks, circling his chopsticks over my flesh. An empty dish.

"We haven't finished the ginger," Lady Jasmine says, and something in her voice sends a little thrill of anticipation through me. The ginger is merely a condiment. I suspect she has something else in mind.

Ayame carries the little dish over to them. She gently lifts out one thumb-sized piece with a clean pair of chopsticks. For a moment I think she is going to feed it to our guests, but then she lays the thin slice over my left nipple. I almost gasp at the unexpected cold shock of it, but I manage to keep silent and still. A minute shudder is all the reaction I allow myself to the intense stimulation. She places a slice on my right nipple, and again I resist the urge to respond.

I lie still and obedient, a good little platter, while they admire the way the ginger clings to the hard buds of my nipples like sheer, wet silk. But Ayame isn't finished. My heart pounds in my ears as she moves down to my splayed and bound legs.

"Perhaps a little wasabi as well," she says. She meets my eyes as she says it, a mischievous smile playing on her lips. Then she dabs a larger slice of ginger into the little ball of green wasabi. Immediately I imagine the taste of the hot green mustard and the tang of pickled ginger. But Ayame doesn't intend for anyone to eat the combination. Carefully she maneuvers the spicy morsel between my open legs, drawing it gently up the dewy crease of my lips before pressing it firmly against me. She pats it into place with her chopsticks, sending little electric jolts through my body. Then she steps back and waits.

For a moment I feel nothing. I know how both would taste in my mouth, and I try not to imagine the same burn in such a tender area. Before long I don't have to imagine it. It begins as a soft, warm tingle, almost a vibration, then builds slowly to a steady burn. My sex clenches in response, but this only intensifies the prickly heat. It's all I can do not to squirm and roll my hips.

"She's very good, isn't she?" the man says admiringly. "Very well trained."

I close my eyes, taking pride in his words as I try to focus on anything but the building heat in my sex.

"Oniyuri is one of our best girls," Ayame says, playing her chopsticks up and down along my inner thighs, teasing me.

Lady Jasmine follows her lead, circling my right nipple with her chopsticks. After several agonizing seconds she captures the slice of ginger and lifts it to her mouth. Her husband follows suit and my nipples ache from the peppery feel of the ginger, the teasing and denial. My skin has never felt so alive, and my composure has never been so challenged.

The tingling warmth between my legs is building to a powerful burn I'm trying desperately not to respond to. I press my toes together, using muscles the guests can't see to distract me from what is fast becoming very intense.

The man gazes down at my breasts. Then he lowers his chopsticks to my nipple, pinching it like a bite of salmon roe. He manipulates the chopsticks gently, rolling the sensitive skin between them and exerting pressure. When Lady Jasmine does the same I have to bite back a little whimper. The sensation is almost too much. My skin tingles all over with the stimulation, raising gooseflesh and making me tremble.

And when Ayame presses her chopsticks against the last piece of ginger, intensifying the contact with my delicate sex, I can't help it. I cry out.

Immediately the room is silent, heavy with disapproval. I choke back a sob, along with the urge to beg forgiveness, to ask for another chance to prove my complete obedience, my training and my ability to endure. But I know it is too late.

"Oh dear," Ayame says softly, and the subtle reproach from her is the worst torment of all.

She plucks the ginger from my nether lips, but the sting is not lessened by its removal. If anything the sudden current of air heightens it. I moan softly, my control already lost.

Lady Jasmine shakes her head sadly. "And she was doing so well."

"Yes," her husband says with a sigh, and I know exactly what he's going to say next. "She will have to be punished."

A hot blush floods my face at his words, and my sex pulses in response. He stands over me, his chopsticks in one hand. He holds them loosely at the widest end while with his other hand he pulls the tips slowly back as though drawing a bow and arrow. The suspense is its own special torment as I hold my breath, waiting. At last he lets go and the tips flick down across my breast, striking the sensitive nipple with perfect aim. I yelp at the sudden sharp pain, all pretence of silence and serenity abandoned.

He leans forward and repeats the treatment on my right breast, making me hiss with pain. I barely have time to process it before he returns to the other side to deliver another stinging stroke. I writhe on the table, but the ropes hold me firmly in position. All I can do is whimper and grit my teeth as the makeshift implement whips my tender breasts again and again, striking like a snake. And even as each stroke elicits cries and vain struggling from me, I find myself admiring his precision and my sex throbs with the excitement of his absolute control. I have no idea how many times the slender little chopsticks deliver their sharp bite but my nipples are sore and inflamed when he finally moves away.

But he isn't finished with me.

He gazes down at my sex, presented like an offering in its frame of orchids. And when he aims the chopsticks again I gasp and yank at the ropes binding my legs. There is no escape, however, and I am helpless as he aims a cruel stroke down across the swollen knot of my clit. My sex explodes with sensation, every nerve ending wildly alive and burning with wanton excitement, the pleasure all the more stimulating for the pain. Lady Jasmine and Ayame watch, their eyes glittering with pleasure at my situation.

I close my eyes, feeling each sharp stroke more intensely than the last. Exhilarated, I writhe helplessly in my red silk bonds, gasping and crying out with complete abandon. Before long I feel myself climbing, my sex throbbing with desire so intense it soon becomes unbearable. I barely realize it when the punishment ends. My body resonates for long moments after the last stroke, savoring the echo of the torment. Lady Jasmine presses her cool fingers against my burning nipples the climax breaks over me like a wave and I throw back my head with a wild animal cry.

Sharp, hot little pulses surge through my body, swelling and receding, making me dizzy. There is the sensation of floating, of flying, of falling. I feel both detached and profoundly connected to my body and all its tumultuous sensations. I can hear voices, the rush of blood in my ears, the distant *shamisen*. The taste of salmon is still rich in my mouth, the scent of jasmine and ginger in my nose. All my senses are on fire.

"Well, well," someone says, the smile evident in his or her voice. Is it my tormenter? His wife? I'm so lost in bliss I can't tell.

But I recognize Ayame's touch as she strokes me softly, as though waking me from a dream. "Oniyuri," she whispers, bending down to kiss me. "It's time for dessert now."

I open my eyes and am a little surprised to see that the guests have resumed their seats. They are watching Ayame expectantly.

With a soft wet cloth she cleans me, wiping away every trace of fish oil, teriyaki and soy sauce. I sigh with pleasure at her cool, gentle touch. My skin tingles with the memory of pain even as it savors this new pleasure. When she is done she dips her fingers into a little bowl and sprinkles my body with powdered sugar. It falls like a light dusting of snow. Onto the newly prepared surface Ayame arranges little scoops of green tea ice cream. My body is so warm it begins to melt almost at once but I still strive not to shiver at the cold.

And as the guests enjoy their dessert I think of winter, of white-capped mountains and icy lakes and a single brazen tiger lily pushing up through the snow, heralding the return of spring.

BLAME *SPARTACUS*

Laura Antoniou

I see them all the time now, blockbuster movies filled with preternaturally handsome twentysomethings masquerading as teenagers in some futuristic dystopia, or manly hunks in skimpy loincloths and sculpted armor hacking away in CGI-rendered stadiums on giant screens or via my deluxe cable-TV package. It's so very chic today, to enjoy tales of epic personal battles for the pleasure of a bloodthirsty audience. This is quite an improvement from the time when the very phrase "gladiator movie" was a not-so-sly comedic reference to homoerotic diversions.

Erotic, yes. And while I appreciate the fact that my gay male friends also enjoy the scenery—and the scenario—I am not a member of that team. I'm straight, if someone as kinky as I am can be called that. And I'm definitely a woman. I can show you proof.

But only once the battle has been fought and won.

I blame *Spartacus*. Specifically, I blame Kirk Douglas. Not that there's anything wrong with the current crop of *Sparticanni*, they are all quite handsome and well worth the subscription to premium channels. But I can remember the exact instant I became alive and aware of my fascination with men who would enter combat for my pleasure.

It was on a Saturday night when I was around fourteen or fifteen, on the threshold between going out with groups of friends and being invited on solo dates. That night, though, I had no planned adventures, and wouldn't have wanted to go if I did. I was home aching with my period, feeling uncomfortable and bloated; tired, cranky and unloved. Flipping channels on television, I saw images stream by second by second, not even really registering anything on my way to find MTV or some other usual distraction. Then, my brain picked up on something and I clicked back and back again...and there he was. A broad-shouldered man with an enormously cleft chin, barely dressed, scuffling with another man in the dust.

I lingered, watched. Even then, there was a spark. My period aside, I was a healthy girl with a solid interest in the male form. One of my girlfriends had shared some pictures she'd found online and saved, in those days before we all had smartphones, on a disk. The two of us eyed the men's bodies with curiosity and immature longing. Men were so much more interesting than boys our own age, we agreed. And for me, unspoken, a little additional twist. Men *who would do what I liked* would be the most interesting of all. What I actually liked was still academic. It was the nature of obedience that turned me on, even back then.

That night, watching the men fight on my television screen, I realized something else.

I liked to watch men grappling with each other.

I kept the television on that channel and wound up watching all of *Spartacus*, the 1960 film directed by Stanley Kubrick.

Oh, it was filled with stars of enormous magnitude! Laurence Olivier! Peter Ustinov! Charles Laughton! Even skinny little Tony Curtis. And while the older, less shapely men draped themselves in bedsheets, the fit and muscular ones stripped down to leg-baring loincloths and leather straps across their upper arms and chests. But even better—they stripped down and picked up weapons and fought each other for the amusement of the better-clothed, aristocratic spectators who wagered on the matches.

I remember holding the remote in my hand, frozen in place, watching the screen flicker. The training regimen; the small dark cells where the gladiators lived, the casual way a woman was thrust into a cell like a hotel housekeeper delivering extra pillows. The different styles of combat—with a short sword and shield, or curved sword and greaves, or spear and net!

Oh. Oh, to be a spectator there, leaning elegantly over my seat to pluck crisp, cold grapes from a tray; to sip blood-red wine while I watched men pant and growl and circle each other like animals. To *own* one of those men and place a coin down while laughing, betting with my friends who would fall first. To see my man, my property win, and take my winnings and take my gladiator home, and...and...

I must have been fourteen. I don't remember actually imagining what would happen beyond kissing him. But in my mind, he would be a much better kisser than Terrance Galbraithe, my on-again, off-again, almost boyfriend.

The gladiatorial fights end early in the movie and then it becomes a vast adventure tale that ends badly for all the slaves. But it didn't matter; I was hooked. I no longer wanted just any good-looking man to populate my nascent fantasies; I wanted a gladiator. I wanted a man who would fight for me, because I told him to. Or because he wanted to please me and gain my favor.

I became a fan of boxing, wrestling and martial arts in

general. Fencing became so much more interesting when I fantasized knights and musketeers dueling for the opportunity to woo me. As my body and tastes and experiences became more mature, my fantasies remained solidly in that realm. And the first time a boyfriend of mine actually did vow to kick the ass of any other boy who looked at me, I must admit it was thrilling for the moment.

And then I decided he was a posturing ass. Shortly after that, I realized I would never actually *experience* this fantasy. I truly didn't want a real man who would go out and hurt someone else and risk harm to himself, arrest, shame and the reputation of a macho jerk. I scolded myself for even harboring such fantasies and tried to write them off as the longings of a girl-child unaware of real-life values. They were as foolish, I decided, as lusting for vampires, or pirates.

Cody is slender and carries himself with the precise grace of a tightrope walker; his unstylishly long hair is fine and colored like honey fresh from the comb, run through with strands of corn silk. He wears it clubbed for Revolutionary War reenactments and most of his friends and coworkers think that's why he has grown it out.

But I love trailing my fingers through it when he is on his knees in front of me or leaning against my leg while I read or watch a movie. I also enjoy watching him run across dusty fields in period uniforms, a Hessian mercenary or a Redcoat. I never lost my taste for costume dramas, and he always has a movie or a series or a book for me and can regale me with folklore and amusing tales like a modern Scheherazade.

And he looks so appealing in the wrestling singlet I ordered for him online, nothing but cobalt-blue Lycra cupping his cock and balls and his sweet, pale ass; with straps framing his body, curling over his shoulders and crossing his back. His stomach and chest are bared for me, shorn even of the light, pale hairs that barely dusted them. Low, light boots are on his feet and a soft suede collar, the same color as the singlet and lined with a layer of brushed cotton, is tight around his neck. It fastens with Velcro, because it's just for decoration. He might earn the chain if he rises victorious.

Cody came in answer to my ad on one of the alternative sex websites. Sorting through dozens of poorly written notes, hundreds of messages from men who hadn't bothered to read my actual ad and thousands of pictures of penises yielded me exactly one man who had lasted beyond my layers of getting-to-know-you filtering. Cody not only wrote complete sentences in English, he addressed me respectfully and included in his first note to me not a picture of his gonads taken while standing at his bathroom mirror, but the shot of him holding a trophy and wearing a *gi*. He had a bruise under one eye and was grinning madly.

He read my ad.

I discovered the world of alternative sex and BDSM where everyone else has—online. Idly browsing one day, I had put "sexy gladiators" into a search engine and expected the usual array of photos from old Italian sword and sandal movies. Instead, I found a gay porn website of men wrestling and then getting it on. The clips I saw had me as frozen in place as my teenage self years ago. But this time, I had a credit card. This time, I could stop the action, and start it again and see the whole thing. Every glistening inch of manly flesh displayed for me in the privacy of my home, as they rolled and grabbed and grunted and growled...and then...

And then they fucked.

Usually the winner got his cock sucked or got to use the loser doggie style, but sometimes that seemed to shift into mutually pleasurable acts. I knew my preference at once. The winner had to get something, yes, but the loser had to *suffer*.

And by the way, I still needed to be in charge. How to manage this took a while to figure out. It took my discovering that I wanted more than an acquiescent lover in my bed. I wanted—I desperately wanted—two men, competing to please me: one to win, and the other to suffer.

For my pleasure. And while there is nothing aesthetically displeasing about watching two men engage in enthusiastic sex with each other, I would prefer that at least one be paying attention to me. While the other suffered.

See the theme?

Alvaro was a furry man, but not with the wiry, bristly, coarse fur I personally find unattractive. His was jet black and straight along his forearms and down his calves, dusted across his chest and then down the center of his hard stomach like a cross, to expand in a bush around his cock and over his balls. I had him clip that area short, but not shave it. The fur there and across his round asscheeks was just as pleasing to me as the silky hair on Cody's head. Alvaro, older than Cody and shorter, was also more stocky and muscular, and the hair on his head was receding. This he also kept short, along with the line of hair along his jaw, a sexy strap of a beard and a mustache to match.

Alvaro did not take me to war-games or regale me with tales of Revolutionary derring-do. But he made me *caldeirada*, brimming with chunks of lobster and whole tiger shrimp, he found rich red wines to entice my palate and rubbed my feet and temples and back with consummate skill, humming lullabies and love songs under his breath.

I met Alvaro at a fetish party; I was in a long black leather gown that laced up the front and sides. He was dressed as a *luchador* from Mexico, only his trunks were black latex, as was the silver-streaked face mask. I asked him if he wrestled in real life as well, and he grinned behind the mask, his teeth showing the gleaming uniformity of crowns. "I wrestle and box!" he told me making a muscle with one firm bicep. "Do you like to watch?"

"Yes," I replied, running a finger down the center of his chest. "Yes, I do."

Tonight I have made Alvaro wear the scarlet singlet, boots and collar. My boys had arrived nice and early. Cody cleaned a bit, moved heavy furniture, sorted out my recyclables and updated my calendar on the computer and my phone. Alvaro roasted potatoes and eggplant and medallions of veal while his wine breathed and flan set. Cody drew my bath and left me soaking to a mix he'd programmed onto my iPod; when I got out, Alvaro met me with a warm towel and soothing almond oil to rub into my skin before I dressed for dinner.

My boys have learned to share as well as compete. I brought them along slowly to understand that my desires cannot be filled by one man; I had to have at least two. Four would be better. But *if* they kept me diverted, then perhaps I could make do with only two.

The heady port served to me after dinner was not nearly as intoxicating as the entertainment to follow. My men, facing each other, dressed as I pleased, eyeing each other warily, ready for my word to begin. Furniture had been moved to create their battleground, leaving me to recline, Roman style, their single spectator.

"Freestyle," I finally said. It might have been Greco-Roman, collegiate or grappling. Alvaro had started judo classes; Cody had taken up boxing. It was my plan to be able to watch them in a mixed martial arts matchup. It was my dream to offer them up as a team against some other gladiatorial-minded collector of fighting men. One day, I will find someone else, I'm sure. In the meantime—they will wrestle for me.

Freed from a formal first position, they each feinted forward immediately, then danced lightly back. Neither one was fool enough to fall for the feint; I found it delightful. I sipped my sweet port and nodded as I watched them circle each other, shoulders hunched, eyes darting, hands flexing.

Cody made the first real move, charging forward in a spear, trying for a double leg pin. But it was far too early and Alvaro turned aside easily and grabbed for Cody's shoulder, propelling him farther and faster and straight down to the floor. Cody hit with a slight stumble and in an instant Alvaro was on top of him looking for a pin.

But Cody was wiry-strong and flexible; he twisted and squirmed and got one elbow braced and bucked back; I could see the tension all through his arms as he put all his strength into pushing Alvaro off of his back. He kicked out one leg and caught Alvaro between his, and in an instant, he rolled and knocked Alvaro off. Pulling his limbs in like a shocked tortoise, he rolled backward and leapt up in a gymnast's move that made me applaud with glee.

Alvaro shot an arm out to try and grab Cody's ankle, but Cody leapt out of the way and then dived down to throw his body against Alvaro's. Alvaro was trying to rise, and Cody's lighter form slammed against his bowed back, but Alvaro didn't even pause. Cody scrambled to try and grab an ankle, an elbow, but his moves were in vain. Alvaro simply rose to his knees with Cody still draped around him; he reached out and back and found Cody's slender arm and one leg and twisted and grunted and brought the younger man up and then threw him down onto his back!

Oh, bravo, I thought, my eyes wide and my thighs wet. *Yes, pin him now, press him down, flatten him!* Did I cry out loud? Sometimes I did. Sometimes, it all stayed in my head, along with the roars of the stadium behind me.

They squirmed and struggled together. Alvaro's buttocks shook and clenched as he tried to pin the ever-moving sinuous body beneath him. Cody planted his boots and arched his back and then brought one knee up sharply, slamming Alvaro in the hip.

"*Caralho!*" Alvaro exclaimed with a tooth-baring grimace. In flinching, he lost his hold on Cody's legs and the lithe younger man twisted like an eel and sprang back, panting.

"Yeah, fuck you too," Cody snarled.

Alvaro darted forward to grab one of Cody's legs, but he was off balance and breathing hard. Cody hip-checked him and tried a toss, but Alvaro's weight and strength didn't allow for an easy lift. Cody gasped as his lift failed and Alvaro laughed and shoved his back against Cody's chest, crowding him toward the center of the room. Cody took the shove and was already slightly off balance when Alvaro elbowed his way inside his defenses and slammed him down hard onto his back, Alvaro splayed over him.

Alvaro didn't stay there, though; he hammered that elbow back one more time, forcing the breath from Cody's mouth, and then turned and grabbed him and lifted one leg while pressing his shoulder down.

"One," I said idly, running a finger down the front of my blouse. My nipples were hard enough to ache. "Two..."

Cody tried kicking, he tried squirming and he slapped his free arm against the floor in frustration. Baring his teeth again, he growled and fought, but Alvaro stubbornly set his muscles and weight against him and would not be moved.

"Done!" I pronounced.

Alvaro immediately let him go and Cody cursed, his fists tight, face flushed with the shame of being beaten, the frustration of loss. Now my own hunger grew like a wild thing; caged for the civilized courses, let free in the darkness of my fantasies. Were those tears, or beads of sweat on Cody's pink face? Either would please me, but both made my body ache with need.

"Again," I said. Waiting would make my play sweeter. "Greco-Roman. Begin."

Quickly, they shuffled, took the first neutral position and moved in on each other looking for an arm drag. Now there could be no leg grabs, nothing below the waist. This left their clenched asses flexing under the iridescent stretching material of the singlet, their unfettered cocks and balls bundled loosely and exposed as clearly to me as though they were out and dangling. I had seen versions of the singlet with a hole for a man's package to poke through, and had occasionally considered buying some. But there was a visual pleasure in watching their flesh so barely contained by that sheer fabric, noticing the appearance of a hard-on or the absence of one. Alvaro, I noticed, had a few drops of moisture making a darker spot on his gladiatorial uniform.

That was because he had won. I watched them slip in and out of grips on their upper arms and shoulders, like some strange, angry dance, and selected a thin chocolate from the plate next to me. In the split second of my attention being drawn away, Cody darted in, grabbed Alvaro's left wrist and pulled, hard, and turned in a neat, economical circle. Alvaro seemed to be able to follow through toward recovery, but then he stumbled, and Cody immediately pushed that same arm and leapt forward, adding extra force and momentum to the move. Alvaro went down so quickly all I saw was a flash of his boots, and then

Cody was on top of him, spreading his arms and keeping his legs away from any pinning position.

Such a good boy!

"Bravo!" I finally said aloud. "Cody, take the bottom position."

His grin of victory quickly vanished; Alvaro was better on the bottom, having more strength. But Cody needed the practice. He got onto his hands and knees, shaking his head and blinking; Alvaro quickly got into the reverse lock position, tucked alongside Cody's body, facing his ass. Taking a deep breath, he leaned over the younger man and locked his hands around Cody's waist. I took a slow, deep breath. My personal porno channel was right here.

"Begin."

Cody immediately seemed to go limp as he tried to pull his whole body flat to the carpeted floor. This might have lost an opponent the ability to do a simple and clean lift, but Alvaro was ready. With every muscle on his beautiful back he strained and pulled and plucked Cody up off the floor and into the air. Cody tried not to engage his legs in fighting back—if he kicked Alvaro, he'd lose right there—and in his panicked distraction could do nothing but grimace as Alvaro rotated his powerful shoulders and slammed him back onto the floor. It was a beautiful move: perfectly executed, skilled and savage.

Did I have it in me to wait for one more pin? My nipples said no. The way the wine had gone to my head and the chocolate melting on my fingers—had I forgotten to eat it?—told me no.

And I didn't have to wait. They were my gladiators.

I extended my chocolate-smeared fingers and beckoned to Alvaro. "Look what you've done," I said. "Had me so mesmerized I wasted my chocolate. Clean that." He eagerly took my fingers into his mouth and suckled and licked, panting around them as he tried to control his breathing. I withdrew them, and wiped them idly on the strap of his singlet. "Bring me three things," I said, leaning back on one elbow. "For Cody."

Cody had already brought himself to his knees, his face a mask of disappointment and shame. I breathed in the scent of his body and shook my head. "You must learn to win from the bottom," I said, pleased that he'd lost. Last time, he'd taken Alvaro down in two out of three matches before my lust declared him the winner and interrupted the match. He'd chosen a butt plug, a cock cage and a whip. Silly boy. Alvaro had liked all three.

And he had his revenge at last. For he returned with a slightly larger toy meant for insertion—one of those vibrators that shimmied and wiggled. I had found it too distracting to use for my own pleasure and had thrown it into my toy box without remembering it for some time now. Also in his hand was a pair of clamps with weights and a blindfold.

Oh, clever Alvaro. Now Cody wouldn't even be able to watch.

I beckoned to Cody and handed him the garishly colored vibrator. "I suggest you put a condom on this and lubricate it before you present your ass to me." He nodded and whispered, "Yes, Ma'am," before he took it and scampered off.

"And what shall we do with you tonight?" I said aloud, rising to allow Alvaro to undress me. "What has tonight's champion earned?"

"A kiss?" he teased, confident and proud. His cock jutted out like a horn, stretching the thin Lycra so much I could see the wrinkles made by his foreskin. I ran a finger neatly along each strap of the singlet and they fell down his arms and the garment bunched around the bottom of his ass. He drew my blouse off gently and unzipped my skirt.

Cody sucked in a breath as he came back into the room on

his hands and knees. The controller box for the vibrator was tucked behind one of the straps of his singlet. So, he was being a clever boy as well!

Right then, I could have fucked them both. But rules were rules, especially when they were my rules. Cody lost. And now, he would suffer.

So he only saw my nakedness for a few seconds before I strapped the blindfold on. Then I put him on his knees with a pillow up between his legs to help keep that vibrator where it was so snugly fitted. I put a clamp on each nipple and then clipped a weight, letting them bounce lightly in my fingers before releasing them. Then, my own touch, I used the thin cord I kept around just for occasions such as these and put a slipknot around the head of his cock. Disgraced or not, it was semi-hard, full of blood and stiffening at my slightest touch. Pulling it free of the singlet, I pressed the pale, curved column against his stomach and placed the end of my little cock leash in his teeth.

"Don't lose that," I whispered to him, as I found the controller box for the vibrator. I switched it on and heard the tiny little engine inside start to buzz. Cody jerked as it moved inside him and moaned around the cord in his teeth.

"Next time, you will fight harder," I said, not sure whether it was a command, a threat or an observation. Then I turned back to Alvaro.

"So, gladiator, have you earned the right to pleasure me?" I asked. I stood over him like the conqueror I was—owner of male flesh and bone, director of my own games. He looked up at me from his knees, his eyes bright and cock rampant.

"Keep that nice and hard," I cautioned him, as I slipped back onto my couch, one knee up, one leg down. I spread myself wide for him, a reward and a command and a threat and a promise. "Kiss me now, champion. Kiss me until I am ready to use that weapon you've got there and maybe I'll allow you a victory orgasm yourself tonight."

He crawled forward, even though he could have risen; he bowed his head to me one more time before his lips and tongue approached my pussy. He kept his hands away, one no doubt on that rampant cock, but touched me only to give pleasure, as I had taught him. I threw my head back and turned to see poor Cody, shivering and straining, his cock harder now, his hips moving and shaking the weights on his nipples, a circle of sensation and discomfort and shame.

I looked back and forth between the two, fortunate and tormented, rewarded and punished and both mine, all mine. My impatience rose again and I laughed in the shuddering after-shocks of my first orgasm. Reaching for a condom, I tossed it onto the floor next to the couch, then grabbed Alvaro's hair and kept his mouth pressed against me. "Again," I purred, in between gasps. "Again, one more time, maybe two and then my champion, maybe I'll use that cock..."

But there was no maybe about it. My men. My gladiators. My pleasure. I was the ultimate winner of every match, the way I always dreamed it might be.

Now, if I could only find out where one learned to fight with a trident and a net....

CLOSE SHAVE

Alison Tyler

There was no reason on earth for me to enter the barbershop. I'm a girl, after all, and this place was clearly for men only. Not that there was a sign stating the rules—one of those internationally understood outlines adorning bathroom doors. But the attitude was drenched in testosterone. In the window, a cactus grew obscenely out of a ceramic pair of pants—a prickly penis, if you will. Old *Playboys* died faded deaths on the sun-drenched table. Shiny retro barber chairs stood in a row like good little soldiers.

But none of that mattered.

I only wanted him.

Whenever I closed my eyes, there he was. A relic, like those chairs. Good looking in an old-fashioned way that suited the place. He had black, slicked-back hair. Sailor Jerry tattoos on his forearms. A razor strop hanging from his station. He did men's cuts and shaves. With a fluffy brush and warm towels. Like in the old days—old days long before he was born.

I had no reason to enter the barbershop, but I stepped inside when I knew he'd be by himself. I'd walked by the shop often enough to have memorized the hours he worked.

He glanced around helpfully. Obviously, I'd come into the wrong place. I couldn't be looking for my boyfriend or husband because there was nobody else there. I couldn't be looking for a cut, because I was a woman. That's what his eyes told me in the split second of silence between us. But I took a deep breath and sat in his chair.

"Ma'am—" he started.

"Oh no. Don't 'ma'am' me," I said quickly. "I'm not married."

"Miss—" he tried next.

I shook my head. "Miss" was too young. Too girly. And here I was, about to ask for a shave.

"We're not one of those...those *unisex* salons." There. He'd done his job. He'd warned me off. He waited for me to climb out of his chair, apologize for my error, be on my way.

"I don't want unisex," I said, "but I *do* want sex."

He met my eyes in the mirror. I didn't look away.

"I'm here by myself," he said.

"I don't want to fuck the two old guys," I told him, explaining what I thought was obvious. "I want to fuck you."

He had to laugh. "Those old guys are my dad and my uncle."

"Then it's a good thing they're not here," I said. "Or maybe I'd get you in trouble." I eyed the strop. He saw where I was looking.

"*I* wouldn't be the one to get in trouble," he said. "You're talking like a girl who needs to be taken out behind the wood-shed."

Those words let me know I'd chosen correctly. This was the right man. He would give me what I needed. But then he looked at the clock on the wall above the mirrors and said, "You have to go."

I didn't budge. I had saved up all my self-confidence for this moment. I was not leaving without the correct change.

He licked his lip. He was wavering. I could feel his will begin to shake.

"I've seen you," he said.

I nodded. "Twice a day. When I walk that way to work." I pointed. "And that way home."

"You always glance inside."

"Always," I agreed.

"Come back later. Tonight. Nine o'clock."

I slid out of the chair. Then I leaned up on my tiptoes and kissed him. There was that cactus erection in the window, men's magazines featuring girls who had gotten their implants long before I'd lost my training wheels, and then there were the two of us. He kissed me back, almost in spite of himself, and said. "You have to go."

"I'll see you at nine. For my shave."

I winked at him before hurrying from the shop.

I'd been planning this tryst for months. I'd learned everything I could about Tommy. I knew he wasn't seeing anyone. My coworker Chelsea was friendly with his sister. She had told me about the women he dated. Those goody-two-shoes types who fit the cookie-cutter mold of what ladies' magazines tell us of how women are supposed to behave. That wasn't me. I'd never be one of them. I'd given up trying a long time ago.

But I knew I was his type. His real type. All I wanted was for him to spread shaving cream all over my pussy and zip away the fur with a razor. I wanted to feel the warm towels after. And then—oh yes—I wanted to feel his tongue.

Chelsea had told me he only dated girls his family approved of. Chelsea insisted I would never get that nod of approval. I didn't care about any of that. I only wanted him.

When I returned at nine, the store was closed. The sign said so, hanging off-kilter in the door. But I didn't believe the sign. I saw a light on in the back, and I opened the door, the bell overhead jangling to announce my entrance. Tommy walked in from the rear, and he didn't seem surprised to see me, but he did seem pleased.

"What did you mean about the shave?"

On the table was a bottle of wine and two glasses. I hadn't noticed that before. He lowered the shades and I poured myself some red. The *Playboys* were gone, too. He'd cleaned up the place for me.

"I mean," I said, "a shave." I sat on the leather couch in front of the coffee table, and I spread my legs.

"This isn't happening," he said.

I hiked up my skirt. "You do shaves," I said. "I need a shave."

"You need to put some panties on is what you need to do. This isn't how girls are supposed to behave."

"I'm not the kind of girl who behaves," I said.

He seemed torn for a minute. And I was thrilled when he walked to my side and dragged his thumb roughly between my pussy lips. Swollen. Juicy. He licked his thumb and looked at me, and then he said, "This isn't how things work."

"No? Not in the boys' world? Where the men call the shots?"

"Not in *my* world," he said, defensively. "I'm not used to a woman being in charge."

"What are you used to?" I was thinking of the world I'd

grown up in: men smoking out on the stoop and the women in the kitchen. Lace doilies on the backs of armchairs. Framed pictures of faraway places that nobody would ever visit on the walls.

He was the one to surprise me. He sat at my side on the sofa and pulled me over his lap. "I like to take the first step," he said. "Ask the girl out. Take her on a date. Bring her flowers. See if there's chemistry."

"Clearly, there's chemistry," I said to the sofa. "You tasted for yourself."

"But you're so forward," he said. "That can't go unpunished. I mean, I don't even know your name."

My pussy clenched. This wasn't how I'd envisioned the fantasy at all. I'd thought I would shock him, that he would appreciate a girl with a little spunk. But I hadn't expected this—his hand on my ass, delivering a blistering, over-the-knee spanking within moments of me entering his shop.

"Every time you walked past," he said, and he punctuated each word with a slap, "I thought of doing this. Your skirts are too short, do you know that?" He was tanning my hide with his big, strong palm and I couldn't respond. The way my clit felt bumping against his knee was sublime. But finally I managed, "Too short for what?"

"Too short for you own good," he said, and he pushed me from his lap so I was on the floor, looking at him. His erection was outlined beneath his slacks. I started to come forward, so I could undo his fly, release his cock. I wanted to suck him. I could practically feel his cockhead in my mouth. So I was shocked when he pushed me away.

"You know what you need?"

"Your cock."

He grimaced at me, and I said, "Oh, what? Girls in your

world don't say the word *cock?* Or maybe they don't suck it. Wouldn't want to spoil their lip gloss."

"Behind the shed. I was right before. That's what you need. A long hard session with an old leather belt where nobody could hear you cry. Tune you up in no time."

"And then what?" I asked, though my pussy was responding to his words, juices dripping down my thighs. "Then I become one of those airheaded girls with the perfect flip? Someone you can control with a look?"

He shook his head. "I can't see you ever being under control," he said. "I'm sure you'd need a pretty steady diet of discipline."

Had I thought I was wet before? I was making a silky puddle between my legs. But I would not lose my moxie. "And you think you're the man for the job?"

"I'm dead sure of it," he said.

"But what about the girls you date? Those princesses."

"I have a theory about that," he said, and he stood and pulled me to standing, then led me toward the back of the shop. "You know what you can't do?"

I shook my head.

He stopped me in the hall, tilted my chin so I was looking into his eyes. "When I ask you a question, you answer."

"Yes," I said quickly.

"That's not how you answer."

"Yes, Tommy?" I tried, feeling less sure of myself now.

"Oh, so you're clever. You know my name, and I don't know yours."

"I'm Janie," I said. "Jane."

"All right, Janie." He looked stern, like I'd disappointed him. "You, with all your tricks, all your fancy plans. You don't even know what you need." He pushed me down then once more, so I was on my knees gazing up at him. "When we're alone, like this, I'm going to be in charge. And you're going to do what I say. So you say, 'Yes, Sir' or 'No, Sir.' Shall we try again?"

"Yes, Sir," I said, and he continued down the hall with me following after in a crawl. When we'd reached the lounge in back, Tommy stood me up again. "The problem with princesses is that you can't fuck them the way you'd like to. You can't tie them up at night. Or use handcuffs. Or a butt plug. You can't spank them when they're naughty or flog them when they need it. You can't wash the bad words from their mouths with a bar of soap—because they never fucking say bad words."

He was stripping me as he spoke, and I saw that there was a basin of water back here and a stack of towels.

"So I've been thinking—as you have pranced by all spring in those too-short skirts of yours—that I don't need a princess."

And then he had me up on the table on my back and he was spreading thick lotion over my pussy using one of those sexy bristle brushes.

"What I need is a bad girl, like you."

He started to shave me. I closed my eyes. I was in heaven, the way he pinched my nether lips as he worked. The way he paid such careful attention to whisking away every last stray bit of hair. My fantasy had definitely come to life.

"Why do you think I'm a bad girl?" I panted.

"Because you're the exact opposite of every good girl I ever dated. You know, I came this close to getting married last fall." He kept working. I watched him as he focused on me.

"It was…" he said slowly, "a close shave."

I was surprised as he spoke, because I'd almost married a man who wanted a Barbie girl. I'd escaped. Like he had.

When he was done, he used a wet towel to rinse me, and then he used those fluffy towels to dry me off. He tested his work with his tongue, and I said, "If you keep doing that, Sir, I'm going to come." I thought it was the right thing to say.

"Fine," he said, looking up at me with his chin wet with my glossy juices. "And then I'll punish you."

My whole world seemed to freeze as he slid two fingers into my pussy.

"How? How will you...Sir?" I managed to tack on at the end.

"We'll start with my belt."

I sighed. I wanted to feel his belt. Desperately, I wanted to, but I couldn't help but ask, "Why?" I needed to hear the words.

"Why will I punish you? Because you're such a forward, pushy tart. Demanding that I take care of you. Not waiting for me to make the first move."

"You didn't. You never did." I didn't mean to sound accusatory. But I had waited. God, I had waited for months.

"I would have," he said. "I was biding my time."

"You were driving me fucking crazy." I didn't care that I'd forgotten the proper words. I was telling him the truth.

"Maybe that was part of my plan," he said, and then he refocused his attention on my split and I came in a flash; the way he made sweet circles over my clit was too dreamy.

In seconds, while I was still lost in that haze of bliss, he had me flipped and bent over the table. I heard the sound of his belt pulling free from the loops of his slacks, and I tensed my thighs in anticipation of the first blow. My ass was still warm from the hand spanking he'd delivered in the front room. I was pretty, pink and primed.

"What I need," he said, and he stung me with a fierce stroke from the start, "is a girl who can put on a princess act every once in a while so my family will get off my back. A girl who can stifle the four-letter words over a Sunday-night dinner. What do you think?"

"What do you mean, Sir?" I was having a hard time responding.

"Most people I know playact in the bedroom. They try to be all kinky when they're so fucking vanilla. I know who you are. I'm asking you to playact *out* of the bedroom. Pretend you're vanilla when we go have a dinner at my grandmother's house. But be the kinky fucking bad girl you are the rest of the time. Do you think you could do that?"

He was landing the blows steadily now, and I was moaning and writhing, my hips beating against the edge of the table.

"Can you do that, Janie?"

I sucked in my breath, because he'd dropped the belt, and I anticipated what was going to happen next. To my delight, I was right. He had unzipped his fly and he was pressing his cock against me.

"Yes," I said, to two things at once. "Yes, Sir," I said to his query and to his cock. "I can do that."

He was in me then, pushing forward so I felt his cock hammering all the way through me. I was so turned on I could hardly think. His cock was thick and hard and seemed to reach places inside me that hadn't been touched before. And all the time Tommy fucked me, he had his hand wrapped in my hair and he kept whispering the things he was going to do to me. The things he couldn't wait to do to me.

"Oh god," I whimpered. "Oh my fucking god."

"You know, I'll have to wash your mouth out when I get you home."

"Why, Sir?"

"Because you can't seem to go two seconds without saying the word 'fuck.'"

"No, Sir, I fucking can't," I said as he made me come a second time. Tommy slammed into me even faster after that, thrusting so hard he moved the table, and us with it, several feet forward. Then he pulled out and came all over my backside, rubbing his semen into my heated skin with the palm of his hand.

After, he washed me with a damp towel and dried me once more. Then he cleaned up the back room while I got dressed. I followed around after him, watching as he returned the shop to normal. The faded *Playboys* in their place. The blinds up.

"Let's go to my place," Tommy said.

"Yes, Sir," I said.

"That's right." He smiled. "Whenever we're with my family, you'll call me Tommy," he said as he led me to his car. "And you'll wear a decent-length skirt and a pair of panties. But don't worry, little girl, when I get you home after, I will take care of you. Exactly how you need."

He stopped at his car and lifted my skirt. He ran his palm over my mound and smiled.

"What do you think?" he asked. And I thought about everything I'd gone through to make it to this point. The waiting. The hoping. The near-disaster of an almost-tragic marriage. I'd survived a close shave, only to be given a kind I'd never truly believed possible.

"Yes, Sir," I said, as I got into his car.

ABOUT THE AUTHORS

NIKKI ADAMS lives amid the quiet fields of southern New Jersey. Her work has also appeared in *Best Lesbian Erotica 2013*.

VALERIE ALEXANDER lives in Arizona. Her work has been previously published in *Best of Best Women's Erotica, Best Bondage Erotica* and other anthologies.

LAURA ANTONIOU (lantoniou.com) has been writing erotica for over twenty years. Best known for her *Marketplace* series, she has also lectured at over 100 events worldwide. Her most recent novel, *The Killer Wore Leather*, is a comedy murder mystery set within the leather/BDSM world.

LAILA BLAKE (lailablake.com) is a linguist, currently working as a writer and translator in her hometown of Cologne, Germany.

She has yet to find a genre to settle down with, but is most dedicated to romance and erotica. Her first novel *By the Light of the Moon* was released in April 2013.

Author and award-winning editor **ELIZABETH COLDWELL** lives and works in London. Her stories have appeared in numerous anthologies including four previous volumes of the *Best Women's Erotica* series. She can be found at *The (Really) Naughty Corner,* elizabethcoldwell.wordpress.com.

LUCY DEBUSSY lives in Edinburgh, where she writes vintage-style smut and sailor porn from a garret in the center of the city. Her writing has previously appeared in *Erotic Review.* She loves circus, dance, sailing, food, silk clothing and good unwholesome erotica.

ROSE DE FER's story "Snowlight, Moonlight" appears in *Red Velvet & Absinthe.* She has published a novella, *Lust Ever After* (Mischief Books) and stories in the anthologies *Underworlds, Submission* and *Forever Bound.* Rose lives in England with her husband, who keeps the chains tight when the moon is full.

As a thoroughly bad girl on a journey of self-discovery as an erotic writer, **TAMSIN FLOWERS** (tamsinflowers.com) is as keen to entertain her readers as she is to explore every aspect of female and male sexuality. She is published by Cleis Press, Go Deeper Press, Xcite Books and House of Erotica.

ERRICA LIEKOS finally realized she could write whatever filthy things she wanted so long as she used a pseudonym. Don't tell her kids. She occasionally Tweets @_Errica and blogs at cumisnotaverb.blogspot.com.

INGRID LUNA is a painter, musician and writer who lives in a little cottage covered with flowers, art and dirty dishes. She loves her kinky husband, the smell of old books, conversations that keep you up all night and hosting parties where everyone gets naked.

SOMMER MARSDEN's been called "...one of the top storytellers in the erotica genre" (Violet Blue) and "Unapologetic" (Alison Tyler). Her erotic novels include *Restless Spirit, Boys Next Door, Learning to Drown* and the *Zombie Exterminator* series. Current addictions include strong coffee, sweet wine, yoga and things that give her goose bumps. Visit her at sommer-marsden.blogspot.com.

CATHERINE PAULSSEN's (catherinepaulssen.com) stories have appeared in *Best Lesbian Romance 2012* and *2013, Best Erotic Romance 2013, Girl Fever, Duty and Desire* (all published by Cleis Press), in Silver Publishing's *Dreaming of a White Christmas* series and in anthologies by Ravenous Romance and Constable & Robinson.

OLEANDER PLUME recently made the transition from writing conventional fiction to erotica, and hasn't looked back. She was recently surprised and delighted to find out that one of her creations has been accepted into a collection of gay erotic short stories, which will be published later in the year.

RUBY RYDER pursues her passion for pegging on her site *Pegging Paradise*. She lives in Southern California, teaches pegging classes to interested couples and is immersed in exploring dominance and submission in conjunction with pegging. She watches porn on the Internet to get in the mood to write her stories.

ALYSSA TURNER (alyssaturnerwrites.blogspot.com) writes erotica and erotic romance in all lengths, having previously been featured in *Best Women's Erotica,* edited by Violet Blue, and several anthologies from Rachel Kramer Bussel. Alyssa has several full-length novels under her belt and no two of her stories are the same.

ALISON TYLER (alisontyler.blogspot.com), the "Trollop with a Laptop," has written twenty-five erotic novels and edited more than sixty erotic anthologies including *Twisted, Torn* and *Smart Ass.* In all things important, she remains faithful to her partner of seventeen years, but she still can't choose just one perfume.

JADE A. WATERS (jadeawaters.com) began her literary naughtiness when she convinced a boyfriend that the sexiest form of foreplay was reading provocative synonyms from a thesaurus. She's been penning erotic tales in Northern California ever since. Her latest piece, "The Flogger," can be found in *The Big Book of Orgasms* from Cleis Press.

ABOUT THE EDITOR

VIOLET BLUE (tinynibbles.com, @violetblue) is an award-winning author and editor, CNET reporter, CBSi/ZDNet blogger and columnist, a high-profile tech personality and one of *Wired*'s Faces of Innovation. She is regarded as the foremost expert in the field of sex and technology, a sex-positive mainstream media pundit (*MacLife*, CNN, "The Oprah Winfrey Show") and is interviewed, quoted and featured in outlets ranging from ABC News to the *Wall Street Journal*.

Blue was the notorious sex columnist for the *San Francisco Chronicle*. She has been at the center of many Internet scandals, including Google's "nymwars" and Libya's web domain censorship and seizures—*Forbes* calls her "omnipresent on the web" and named her a Forbes Web Celeb. She headlines and keynotes at global technology conferences including ETech, LeWeb, SXSW: Interactive and two Google Tech Talks at Google, Inc. and received a standing ovation at Seattle's Gnomedex.

The *London Times* named Violet Blue "one of the 40 bloggers who really count."

Best Erotica Series

"Gets racier every year."—*San Francisco Bay Guardian*

Best Women's Erotica 2013
Edited by Violet Blue
ISBN 978-1-57344-898-7 $15.95

Best Women's Erotica 2012
Edited by Violet Blue
ISBN 978-1-57344-755-3 $15.95

Best Women's Erotica 2011
Edited by Violet Blue
ISBN 978-1-57344-423-1 $15.95

Best Bondage Erotica 2013
Edited by Rachel Kramer Bussel
ISBN 978-1-57344-897-0 $15.95

Best Bondage Erotica 2012
Edited by Rachel Kramer Bussel
ISBN 978-1-57344-754-6 $15.95

Best Bondage Erotica 2011
Edited by Rachel Kramer Bussel
ISBN 978-1-57344-426-2 $15.95

Best Lesbian Erotica 2013
Edited by Kathleen Warnock.
Selected and introduced by
Jewelle Gomez.
ISBN 978-1-57344-896-3 $15.95

Best Lesbian Erotica 2012
Edited by Kathleen Warnock.
Selected and introduced by
Sinclair Sexsmith.
ISBN 978-1-57344-752-2 $15.95

Best Lesbian Erotica 2011
Edited by Kathleen Warnock.
Selected and introduced by Lea DeLaria.
ISBN 978-1-57344-425-5 $15.95

Best Gay Erotica 2013
Edited by Richard Labonté.
Selected and introduced by Paul Russell.
ISBN 978-1-57344-895-6 $15.95

Best Gay Erotica 2012
Edited by Richard Labonté.
Selected and introduced by
Larry Duplechan.
ISBN 978-1-57344-753-9 $15.95

Best Gay Erotica 2011
Edited by Richard Labonté.
Selected and introduced by
Kevin Killian.
ISBN 978-1-57344-424-8 $15.95

Best Fetish Erotica
Edited by Cara Bruce
ISBN 978-1-57344-355-5 $15.95

Best Bisexual Women's Erotica
Edited by Cara Bruce
ISBN 978-1-57344-320-3 $15.95

Best Lesbian Bondage Erotica
Edited by Tristan Taormino
ISBN 978-1-57344-287-9 $16.95

* Free book of equal or lesser value. Shipping and applicable sales tax extra.
Cleis Press • (800) 780-2279 • orders@cleispress.com
www.cleispress.com

Ordering is easy! Call us toll free or fax us to place your MC/VISA order.
You can also mail the order form below with payment to:
Cleis Press, 2246 Sixth St., Berkeley, CA 94710.

ORDER FORM

QTY	TITLE	PRICE

SUBTOTAL _____

SHIPPING _____

SALES TAX _____

TOTAL _____

Add $3.95 postage/handling for the first book ordered and $1.00 for each additional book. Outside North America, please contact us for shipping rates. California residents add 9% sales tax. Payment in U.S. dollars only.

* Free book of equal or lesser value. Shipping and applicable sales tax extra.

Cleis Press • Phone: (800) 780-2279 • Fax: (510) 845-8001
orders@cleispress.com • www.cleispress.com
You'll find more great books on our website

Follow us on Twitter @cleispress • Friend/fan us on Facebook